TEN SECONDS TOO LATE

Samantha Baca

Dark Shadows Series

Five Steps Ahead
Ten Seconds Too Late
Against The Clock

Copyright © 2022 by Samantha Baca.

All rights reserved.

If you are reading this book and did not purchase it, this book has been pirated and you are stealing. Please delete it from your device and support the author by purchasing a legal copy.

All rights reserved. No part of this book may be reproduced or transmitted in any form or by any means, electronic or mechanical, including photocopying, recording, or by information storage and retrieval system, without written permission of the Publisher, except where permitted by law. This book is a work of fiction. Names, places, characters, and incidents are the product of the author's imagination or are used fictitiously.

Cover Design: Richard Baca
Image(s): DepositPhotos

Contents

One: Elena..1
Two: Elena - 14 Days Ago.................................5
Three: Trevor - 12 Days Ago.............................15
Four: Elena - 12 Days Ago................................19
Five: Trevor - 12 Days Ago...............................23
Six: Elena - 10 Days Ago..................................29
Seven: Elena - 9 Days Ago...............................33
Eight: Trevor - 9 Days Ago...............................39
Nine: Elena - 8 Days Ago.................................43
Ten: Trevor - 7 Days Ago..................................51
Eleven: Elena - 6 Days Ago..............................59
Twelve: Trevor - 6 Days Ago............................63
Thirteen: Elena - 6 Days Ago...........................67
Fourteen: Trevor - 5 Days Ago.........................77
Fifteen: Elena - 5 Days Ago..............................83
Sixteen: Trevor - 4 Days Ago...........................91
Seventeen: Elena - 4 Days Ago.......................99
Eighteen: Elena - 3 days Ago.........................107
Nineteen: Trevor - 3 Days Ago......................117
Twenty: Elena - 3 Days Ago...........................129
Twenty One: Trevor - 3 Days Ago..................135
Twenty Two: Elena - 2 Days Ago...................141
Twenty Three: Trevor - 2 Days Ago...............153
Twenty Four: Elena - 2 Days Ago..................159
Twenty Five: Trevor - 1 Day Ago....................165
Twenty Six: Elena - 1 Day Ago.......................171
Twenty Seven: Trevor - 1 Day Ago................177
Twenty Eight: Elena - 8 Hours Ago................189

Contents

Twenty Nine: Trevor - 7 Hours Ago..................193
Thirty: Elena - 4 Hours Ago..................197
Thirty One: Trevor - 1 Hour Ago..................201
Thirty Two: Elena..................207
Thirty Three: Elena..................213
Thirty Four: Elena..................219
Thirty Five: Trevor..................225
Thirty Six: Elena..................227
Thirty Seven: Trevor..................231
Thirty Eight: Elena..................235
Thirty Nine: Trevor..................239
Forty: Elena..................241
Forty One: Trevor..................247
Forty Two: Elena..................249
Forty Three: Elena..................253
Forty Four: Trevor..................257
Forty Five: Elena..................263
Forty Six: Trevor..................267
Forty Seven: Elena..................269
Forty Eight: Trevor..................273
Forty Nine: Elena..................275
Fifty: Trevor..................283
Fifty One: Elena..................291
Fifty Two: Trevor..................295
Fifty Three: Elena - 2 Weeks Later..................299
Epilogue: Trevor - 6 Months Later..................309
Acknowledgments..................315
About the Author..................317
Other Books by Samantha..................319

One
Elena

I chewed my nail as I clutched my glass of wine to my chest, unable to pry my eyes away from the TV as the woman desperately tried to run after the man who had taken her child. She was determined, but I could already tell that he was faster and stronger than her. That's how it always played out. No matter how strong the woman is, there's always a predator that will overtake her. My stomach soured as I thought back to when I had been kidnapped and held captive. I wasn't sure that I would ever escape; each day that passed made it less likely.

A knock on the door startled me, and I flung my arms in the air, sloshing the wine out of the glass. I gasped and set it down on the coffee table before I got up to grab a towel from the kitchen. I patted my arms and chest dry and then tossed the towel in the sink when there was another knock.

I looked through the peephole, my heart still racing from the movie. Whoever was there had their face turned away from me, keeping me from seeing who they were. I was about to walk away and grab my phone when they turned around, and I finally saw their face. Letting out a shaky breath, I turned the lock and slid the deadbolt to open the door.

"Hey, I thought you had to work late?" I stepped to the side and waited for him to come in. Instead, he lingered at the door with his hands shoved into his pockets, his jaw locked in place.

"Are you okay?" I asked, feeling as if something was wrong.

"Fine."

I pulled my head back slightly and tilted it to the side. Something was *definitely* different about him.

"Have you been drinking?"

"What's it to you if I have been?" His words weren't slurred, but the smell of whiskey was heavy on his breath.

"I'm just a little worried about you. You don't seem like yourself."

"Maybe I'm not."

"Did I do something?" I asked, narrowing my eyes in confusion. This wasn't like him and my skin prickled at the realization.

"I don't know. Did you?"

"What's with the games?" I asked, starting to grow impatient and frustrated. I put my hand on my hip and raised a brow. "If something's wrong, then just tell me. Otherwise, I don't know why you're acting this way." I was acting braver than I felt.

"Does it scare you?"

The icy tone in his voice was more jarring than his actual words.

"No," I said slowly. "You don't scare me."

He paused for a moment, studying me with cold, calculating, dark eyes. Something shifted between us, and I felt the icy chill radiating off of him.

"Are you sure?"

Suddenly, my instincts kicked in, and I took a step back, away from him as he stepped toward me. My heart was racing as panic forced its way through my veins, sending me back into the darkness I felt when I was held captive last year.

I grabbed the side of the door, slamming it shut when he reached out and caught it. His hand wrapped tightly around the wood as he held it. His eyes locked onto mine, forcing a wave of fear to crawl up my spine. I took another step back, desperate to get away from him. He was inside my apartment now, the door still open.

"You're breathing fast. Eyes are dilated. I would bet that your palms are sweaty. Fear is coursing through your body right now, and you're trying to decide whether or not to trust *me* or your instincts that are telling you to *run*."

"Why are you doing this?" I whispered. He knew what I had been through; why would he think this was funny?

"So, which is it, *Elena*?" My name rolled off of his tongue in a way I'd never heard before. "Do you trust me, or are you going to run?"

"Stop it!" I demanded, my fists shaking at my sides. "Just go! Get out of my apartment! We're done." I pulled my shoulders back and tilted my chin up as my body trembled.

"Actually," he laughed, shutting the door. "We're just getting started."

I watched in horror as he slid the deadbolt in place, knowing that no one would be able to get in if needed. My head was spinning, and my body screamed for me to get the hell out of there and call for help, but it was too late.

Two
Elena
14 Days Ago

"Are you nervous about Max and Hannah coming over for dinner?" Trevor asked, sliding his hand across my waist as his chest pressed firmly against my back.

I had been jittery all day—or more like all week—and couldn't explain it. Half of my family was worried that I was stressed out about the one-year anniversary of my kidnapping, while the other half were convinced that I was just overwhelmed with trying to decide whether or not to go back to school in January. I had taken two semesters off and hadn't figured out if it was a temporary break or a permanent one. Finding out that one of your professors was secretly obsessed with their students and kidnapping them would make anyone question whether they really wanted to go back.

The joy of having a big family was that no one was ever in complete agreement, which led to plenty of arguments over who was right without forcing me to have to sit down and actually talk about it with any of them. It's not like they would understand anyway. I knew that the likelihood of encountering another "Adam"—or Professor Wright as I had known him—was slim, but that didn't mean that it was impossible. It was New York City, and stranger things had happened.

"Maybe," I admitted, looking up at him as I rested my head against his chest.

Trevor and I had been secretly dating for a while now, and tonight was the night that we were finally going to tell my brother, Max, and his fiancé, Hannah. This would be nerve-wracking for anyone with an overprotective brother, but it was even more so with an overprotective brother who was a cop and just so happened to be best friends with my new boyfriend. Yeah, this wasn't going to be awkward at all.

I tried to force the thoughts about what could possibly go wrong out of my head before they got there. The last thing I needed was to look like I was more of a mess than I already was. Maybe it was the pressure of letting my family into my personal life, or perhaps it was the fear of what my brother would think when he found out. Either way, my nerves were shot, and I suddenly wished I was old enough to drink a beer without my brother scolding me.

When Trevor and I first started dating, there was this insane chemistry between us that had us practically climbing each other every chance we got. It was passion-filled with trust and this sense of knowing that I could be myself with him without worrying that he would judge me. He knew what I went through when Adam took me and had been there with me every step of the way in my recovery since then, which made it feel weird that I hadn't been able to bring myself to tell him—or anyone—about the odd stuff that had been happening. It wasn't anything extreme, just little things that seemed to mess with my head, and the last thing that I needed right now was for everyone to overreact and try to wrap me in a protective bubble. Again.

I tried to chalk it all up to living on my own for the first time in my life. Plenty of my friends had mentioned how they didn't like being alone, so they found roommates to keep them company. Maybe that was all that this was? I just needed a roommate.

But then again, it felt like I already had one and didn't know who they were. Who else would turn the TV on while I was asleep in the middle of the night or leave the stove on while I was in the shower?

"It'll be fine," he assured me, running his hands up and down my arms. I felt a shiver slip through me as he wrapped his arms tighter around me. Instantly, I felt myself relax into his touch, feeling the comfort he always provided me without even trying.

"What if Max is pissed off when he finds out?" I asked, biting my lip.

"Then he's pissed off." He spun me around and shrugged, locking his arms together around my lower back with his fingers laced together right above my ass.

"He's my brother. And your best friend," I countered. "And a cop!"

"Do you think he's going to arrest me for dating his sister?" he chuckled, the dimples in his cheeks setting in with his beautiful smile.

"It's Max," I sighed. "I wouldn't put anything past him."

The doorbell rang, and I felt my palms start to sweat again.

"Well, it looks like we're about to find out," Trevor said, pulling me in for a quick kiss before he rushed off to answer the door.

I nervously ran a hand down my sweaterdress, wondering

if I looked too dressed up. Was he going to assume that this was a double date? It technically was, but I wasn't sure that I was ready for him to know about us just yet.

"Hey, Hannah, come on in," Trevor said, his voice carrying into the living room. I waited anxiously, listening as I heard them by the front door, hanging up their coats.

"Dinner smells delicious," Hannah commented, coming around the corner. Her eyes lit up when she saw me. "Hey, Elena! I'm so happy you're here!"

And just like that, the stress and anxiety that had been building up quickly evaporated when she pulled me into a hug. Hannah had been dating my brother for almost a year, but it felt like she and I had been sisters forever. Which was a genuine compliment, given that I had five real sisters who I was close to as well.

Hannah had been kidnapped by Adam shortly after I had escaped, and luckily, my brother was able to find her before anything terrible had happened. It created a bond between us that no one else could understand, and for that, I was thankful. Hannah could relate to a lot of things that I felt and was the barrier that I needed with my brother when he got to be too overbearing.

"You look so pretty," she cooed, stepping back but holding onto my arms as she took in my outfit. I smiled sheepishly, thankful for the distraction from the look my big brother was giving me from the entryway.

"Don't worry about him," she whispered. "He was grumpy before we got here. He'll be fine after we eat."

"I don't know about that," I muttered between my teeth as I

walked over to say hi to him.

Trevor had slipped into the kitchen while we were talking and announced that dinner was ready before Max could start questioning why I was there. We sat down at the table, and I made sure that I was tucked between Hannah and Trevor, so Max was directly across from me. I wasn't scared of my brother, but I also had no idea how this would go.

"Alright, dig in," Trevor said proudly, setting a basket of breadsticks on the table between the pan of lasagna and the bowl of salad.

We served ourselves while he poured glasses of water and wine, then sat down. I smiled at him the way I always did, then felt Max's eyes on me and looked away.

"So, Hannah, how's school this semester? Are you almost done?" Trevor asked, guiding the conversation to a safe topic.

"It's good, but I've decided to shift majors." She kept her eyes on Trevor, but I noticed the way her hand gripped the fork tightly as Max's jaw twitched.

"Oh? To what?"

"Forensic science."

I felt my eyebrows pull up in surprise and tried to force my expression to return back to normal before she noticed.

Trevor raised his wine glass and continued to give her his full attention as he took a sip.

"What made you decide to switch from psychology–if you don't mind me asking?"

I loved that he wasn't judgmental like my brother. I could already see the disapproval etched on his face and the tension in his body as he clasped his hands together tightly in front of him on the table.

"Well," Hannah paused. She took a deep breath and glanced at Max. "After what happened last year, I decided that psychology wasn't for me. At first, I thought that it would help if I could understand *why* Adam did what he did, but I've realized that I'm not ready to open that box yet. Instead, I'm redirecting my studies to the area that I'm currently obsessed with, much to *someone's* dismay."

"You're obsessed with forensic science?" I asked quietly, wondering if she had been thinking about the same things that had been stuck in my head for the past year.

She nodded and took a bite of lasagna. She took a drink of water and then looked over at Max again. His face was stoic as he waited for her to go on, not bothering to touch his food.

"For whatever reason, I can't wrap my head around the idea that Adam died. I know that I was there when it happened and that, technically, I saw his body, but my brain has hidden so many of those details for me that it feels like none of it really happened. That *maybe* there's a chance that he didn't really die. For all I know, he's still out there. Just waiting to come back and do it again."

"Hannah, we've been through this," Max sighed, reaching over and gently resting his hand on her arm. "He's dead. He cannot and will not hurt you ever again."

He looked up and locked eyes with me for a moment before adding, "*Either* of you."

My stomach somersaulted as I tried to force the images out of my head. The dark room. The photo shrine. The walls that felt like they were constantly closing in. The blood.

I shivered involuntarily and picked up my fork. My fingers trembled as I forced myself to cut a piece of lasagna and take a bite without drawing any attention to myself. I felt Trevor's hand slide over to gently squeeze my knee and let out the breath I was holding before I took a bite.

"Yes, I know," she shrugged. "But I can't force my mind to accept what it doesn't want to. I know that we've been to his gravesite, but how do I know that it's not some sort of setup? What if it's the body of another person that he killed? What if he faked his own death?"

Max started to say something but clamped his jaw shut and pulled his hand back in frustration.

"I get it," I said to Hannah, ignoring the looks from Trevor and Max. "I often worry that he's not really dead and that he's coming back for me too. It's hard to relax and not feel like you constantly have to protect yourself. It's exhausting on so many levels."

"Thank you," she replied sincerely. "No one else gets it."

"I know."

My therapist and I had been over it countless times, and she knew my triggers before I even noticed them. If someone started to get too close to me, I would put up a wall and force them out. It had happened several times with Trevor and me in the last few weeks. Natalie assured me that it was likely the stress of remembering when I was taken last year and everything that happened after that. She even asked for

Trevor to join us for an extra session so she could speak to both of us and help him understand how he could support me. We talked in great detail about the physical things that could trigger me—like walking up behind me without me noticing, dark rooms, touching my throat, or using any pet names.

We continued with dinner after Trevor graciously changed the subject again to something less stressful. After he and Max finished complaining about the Yankees and other sports-related stuff, I knew that it was getting to the time that we needed to share our news with them. That's what this dinner was for, after all.

"I'll clean up," I offered, getting up from the table and grabbing my plate. I reached over for Trevor's when he reached out and grabbed my hand, stopping me. He set my plate down on his and pulled me onto his lap.

"Leave it; the dishes can wait," he said softly.

I felt the heat quickly spread through my body, flushing my olive-toned skin. My hair was pulled up, which gave everyone a clear view of the blush that was creeping up my neck and onto my cheeks.

I glanced at Max and noticed his brows pulled together as he stared at us.

"Elena and I have something that we wanted to share with you guys." Trevor's hand planted firmly on my knee to keep it from bouncing. "We've been dating for a few months and have decided that it's time everyone knows that we're in a relationship."

"How long is 'a few months'?" Max asked without hesitation.

"Since June."

"June?"

Trevor nodded, keeping his attention on Max while Hannah and I stayed quiet.

"Six months, and you didn't think to say anything before now?" Max cocked his head to the side and narrowed his eyes.

"Elena wanted to wait."

"For what?"

"To make sure you didn't arrest me for dating her."

I was going to kill him for making fun of me, but after Max tilted his head back and laughed, I felt better that Trevor had successfully eliminated some of the tension that was mounting around us.

"I wouldn't arrest you," he teased. "But that doesn't mean that I won't break a bone or two if you hurt her."

"Max!" I scolded, pursing my lips the same way our mother does when she's embarrassed by something we've said.

"What? I don't care if it's Trevor or some other guy—I will break some bones if anyone hurts you."

Except Adam.

That wasn't a fair thought, but I couldn't keep it out of my head. Had Hannah not been taken right after I escaped, I don't know what Max would have done to Adam if he ever found him. But part of me believed that the only reason he killed him *was* because of Hannah.

"Well, I don't see anyone needing any broken bones anytime soon," I joked, wrapping my arms around Trevor's neck. It felt good to have Max know about our relationship, but I dreaded that I still had to tell my parents and sisters about it. Being one of seven kids made it hard to do something without the entire family knowing.

Three

Trevor

12 Days Ago

"So, you survived dinner with Max," Roman chuckled as I walked into the office Monday morning.

"Yeah, it wasn't as hard as I thought it would be. I think Elena was more stressed out about it than I was. But then again, she's just overwhelmed with a lot right now, to begin with."

I set my coffee and bagel down on my desk and pulled off my jacket. Roman and I shared an office with desks across the room from each other and a large window between us. It wasn't the best view since it looked out to the alley behind the gym, but at least it let in some natural light.

"What's going on with Elena?" he asked, leaning back in his chair and propping his feet up on the desk. That was the nice thing about where we worked—it wasn't a professional setting with stuffy suits and ties. It was tennis shoes and workout gear mixed with loud noises and men talking shit while they worked out.

"Honestly, I don't know." I ran a hand through my hair, remembering that I needed to get it cut soon. "She's been really stressed out the past few weeks, and her therapist thinks that there are some underlying feelings that she never dealt with after her attack. It's coming up on a year since it happened, and she thinks that maybe the holidays have triggered her memories of stuff that she had repressed."

"I can relate to that," he sighed.

Roman was officially retired after serving in the Marines as a sniper, and we had had several deep conversations about PTSD and the long-lasting impacts his career has had on his life.

"I don't know what to do for her to make things better. She shuts down anytime we talk about what happened, and I get it. I don't like to talk about it either because I get so mad that I can't see straight. But I feel like she's heading in this downward spiral, and I can't catch her fast enough."

"Have you tried talking to Max about it? Maybe he can talk to her?"

"I haven't been able to before now. He would have asked why I knew so much about his sister and probably would have kicked my ass if he found out that way."

Roman tipped his head back and laughed.

"I would pay to see that."

"Shit," I laughed. "Just because he's a cop doesn't mean that I can't take him."

Laughter filled the room as another voice joined in.

"Oh really? Care to make a wager on that?" Max asked, leaning against the door frame with his arms crossed over his leather jacket. He raised an eyebrow and looked between us.

"I don't think you can afford it," I poked. "Not with the big wedding that Hannah has planned."

He winced and ran a hand down his face.

"She's killing me with the small details," he whined. "I don't care whether the rose petals are pure white or white with little purple veins in them, yet she's upset that I'm not helping her. I helped with the big decisions, like where to have it and what kind of food we should have."

"Didn't she veto you on both?" Roman asked, his fingers tapping together as his hands formed a steeple.

"She sure did." He pushed off of the wall and shook his head. "I don't see why we couldn't do it in my parent's backyard and have a barbeque."

"Because it's a wedding and not a retirement party, you old grump." I laughed and rolled my eyes.

"Well, thankfully, Elena is going by later today to help Hannah with the tiny details that I'm apparently incapable of handling."

She hadn't mentioned anything about it to me, but I wasn't going to bring that up. We weren't at the point that she had to check in with me before she went anywhere or did anything, but I thought that we had at least gotten to the point of sharing the little details of our days with each other. Or at least I had.

"So, since the girls will be hanging out and planning for hours, do you want to meet up and grab a beer after work?"

"Sure," I said, taking a sip of my coffee. "I'll meet you at seven."

He said goodbye and then left, leaving Roman and me to start our workday. The hours flew by, and before I knew it, it was lunch, and I still hadn't heard from Elena. I pulled out my cell phone and sent her a quick text, asking how her day was going.

Two hours later, I still hadn't heard anything from her, and I started to worry. It wasn't like her to avoid me, and I felt the anxiety begin to build that something was wrong and she wasn't okay. I called it a day early and left Roman to close up while I headed to her apartment.

I tried calling her a handful of times, but each one went to voicemail. My pulse was racing as I climbed three flights of stairs, not bothering to wait for the elevator. By the time I got to her floor, I was in full fight or flight mode and barreling to her door. I knocked several times and waited.

After the fifth time of knocking so loud that one of her neighbors opened their door to see what all of the commotion was about, I decided to call Max and ask him to get a key from her landlord to do a welfare check. I just prayed that he got there in time.

Four
Elena
12 Days Ago

I was singing along to Ariana Grande when my front door flew open, and Trevor and Max rushed in. I screamed and clutched the towel around my body, still wet from the shower I had just taken.

"What the hell are you doing?!"

"We came to check on you," Trevor exclaimed, his face showing the stress he was under while Max crept through my apartment in full cop mode, checking for any intruders.

"Why didn't you call?" I raised my brows, as well as my voice, and waited for my heart to find its way back into my chest after they scared the living shit out of me.

"I did. I've been calling and texting you for hours. I stood outside knocking until your neighbor threatened to call the police. Finally, I called your brother and asked him to get a key from the manager so we could check on you."

"I haven't had a single call or text from you all day," I said, rubbing my temples while pinching the top of my towel against my body with my elbows.

Trevor looked at me as if I was crazy before slowly pulling

his phone out of his pocket and showing me the messages he had sent and the calls he had made.

"That's weird," I muttered, walking over to the charger on the end table where my phone was plugged in. I picked it up and pressed the home button, but the screen was black. "It's dead."

It didn't make any sense that it was dead when I had been charging it for over an hour.

Trevor bent down and checked the charger, reaching behind the table to where it was plugged in. He wiggled it loose and then pulled it out. The wires by the plug were completely exposed and frayed.

"This is your charger?" he asked, holding it up in the air.

I reached over and took it from him, looking at the damage.

"It's brand new," I whispered. "I just bought it because my other one stopped working."

"Are you sure this isn't the old one?" he suggested, placing a hand on my shoulder.

"No, I purposely threw that one away. I just bought this one. The package is still on the cou..." I turned to look behind us, and my jaw dropped when I saw the charger still sitting on the counter in the brand new packaging that hadn't been opened.

He reached over and grabbed it, checking the box that it was still sealed inside of.

"I swear—I opened it and changed it before I plugged my phone in."

"It's okay, things happen. I'm just glad that we figured it out before this one started a fire. How long has the wire been exposed like that?"

I shook my head in frustration, knowing that he wasn't going to believe me.

"It's never been like that until now."

His eyes narrowed as he studied me. He was so insanely good-looking that I wanted to wash the worry off of his face and replace it with the smile that lit up his dark chestnut eyes. The eyes that used to look at me with adoration and not concern that I had lost my mind.

"Well, why don't I get the new one plugged in for you while I'm here," he offered, avoiding what I had said. He pulled the table out, holding the lamp steady with one hand while he maneuvered with the other. "Have you eaten today?" he asked over his shoulder as he opened the package and pulled the other charger out.

Why did everyone always assume that strange things happened to me because I was hungry? It wasn't like I got super delirious with low blood sugar and did things that I couldn't remember, yet it seemed to be the fix-all as far as they were concerned. *Elena's a little off today? Give her a Snickers–she'll be fine.*

I hadn't bothered to answer him when Max came out of the guest bedroom and spotted Trevor messing with the charger. Trevor glanced at him over his shoulder and then put the table back where it belonged.

"Her charger was bad, so her phone died," he explained.

Max walked over and looked at the one still in my hand, his

brows furrowed.

"That's the one you've been using? That could have started a fire, Elena," he scolded.

I closed my eyes and slowly forced out the breath that was holding all of the sarcastic things that I wanted to say.

Trevor and Max talked for a few minutes while I stood there, uninterested in their conversation. It was happening more and more lately, the lack of interest in anything. Natalie assured me that it was normal to feel some depression as the memories tried to resurface, but this felt like something else.

I was finally living on my own, and for once, I had never felt more alone than I did now.

Five

Trevor

12 Days Ago

I spun the bottlecap on the table, waiting for Max to finish his phone call. Jon came by and set another round of beers on the table, clearing the empty ones as he walked away.

Max and I had been coming to this bar since it first opened, and Jon had been one of the best bartenders I had ever met. He took the time to get to know people, and he was by far one of the most genuine and kind-hearted men around.

"Get me the update as soon as you have it," Max said, ending his call and putting his phone down on the table. He picked up his beer and took a long drink, the stress of his day being washed away.

"Everything okay?" I asked, not wanting to dive into the conversation I knew we were about to have.

"Yeah," he muttered. "No. I don't know. We had a lead on the guy that's been terrorizing the college, but it looks like it's turning into another dead end."

"Sorry. That sucks."

We sat quietly for a few minutes, drinking our beer and avoiding the elephant in the room. I glanced down at my phone, checking to see if there were any new messages from Elena. Nothing.

Hannah agreed to let Max know as soon as Elena showed up at their apartment and update him again when she left. As far as I knew, they were hanging out and talking about what color to have the toilet water for the wedding. Who knew what kind of details they were getting into.

"So," he said evenly. "Should I be worried about Elena living on her own?"

I knew what he was really asking, and I didn't have an answer for him.

"Honestly, I don't know."

"That cord could have set her apartment on fire."

"I know," I breathed out, feeling the stress from this afternoon still sitting on my shoulders.

"Do you think that it's just her being young and not knowing these things, or do you think that there's something else going on that we need to be worried about?"

I leaned back in my chair, picking at the label that was starting to peel off the bottle. Elena and I had been dating for months, and I had noticed that she was beginning to act differently lately, but I had no idea whether this was a simple accident or if we did need to worry.

It scared the shit out of me when I couldn't get ahold of her. My mind had started to scatter to every worst possible situation that it could come up with. Once I saw that she was okay, I was relieved until I found the charger cable frayed with the wires exposed.

Plenty of people used and abused their electronics, so it wasn't a total surprise that her charger was in bad shape, and that's why she bought a new one. The problem was with *how* she reacted to it. She was surprised to see it; I could tell by the look on her face.

"I think she's a very smart girl and is more than capable of being on her own." I kept my eyes locked on the bottle, avoiding looking at him so he didn't call me on the bullshit that was laced in my words. I believed every word I said; I just didn't trust them right now. Something was going on with her, and I was determined to figure it out.

"But…"

I looked up at him, frustrated that he called me on it.

"But I think something else is going on, and I don't know what it is."

"I know that things are *different* now that you guys are dating," Max said, looking around the room before he continued. "But I need you to know that you can always come to me if something is wrong. She's my baby sister—"

"I know she is," I interrupted, suddenly feeling defensive.

"AND you're my best friend," he continued. "Whatever happens between you guys is your business, but it won't change things between us unless you really fuck up. Then I'll kick your ass, and we'll see about being friends."

He winked, and I felt some of the tension lift from my shoulders.

"You know that I love her, man. I always have. It's just a different type of love now."

"I know," he smiled. "She loves you too."

I felt the smile pull up at my lips, hearing him say it.

"How do *you* know that? She hasn't even told *me*."

"I could tell by how nervous she was at dinner. She wouldn't care what I thought if you guys were just fooling around."

I felt my phone vibrate on the table and looked down to find a text message from her. I sent back a quick reply, asking her to let me know when she got home and if she felt like company.

"Is she heading home?" Max asked, looking at his phone.

"Yeah, did Hannah text you too?"

He nodded with a smile.

"She's a good woman," I said, changing the subject.

"That she is."

"How's she doing with everything?"

"I wish I knew." He shook his head in frustration and spun his empty beer bottle on the table. Jon glanced over and pointed at us before Max shook his head, declining another.

"I'm a detective. I'm supposed to be able to read people, and I can't figure her out. She says that she's fine and that it doesn't bother her that it's coming up on a year since everything happened, but I don't think that it's true."

"Why not?"

"Because so much happened last year. How could she not be upset about it? Her best friend was killed. She was kidnapped and tortured by her own professor. She witnessed his death. We got engaged and moved in together. There's been a lot to cram into a year, and I can't imagine that she's not reminded of these things, just like Elena. I feel like I'm just waiting for both of them to have a breakdown, and I don't know when it's coming."

"Maybe it's not?" I suggested. Hannah had been open about her feelings since everything happened and talked about her best friend, Amber, often. I hadn't noticed the depression or anxiety in her that I had seen over the past few weeks with Elena, but a lot of that probably had to do with their situations and how different they were. Elena had been held a lot longer than Hannah and had tried to escape several times before she was successful. Hannah was found quickly after she was taken and didn't endure the same trauma that Elena did.

"I hope so," Max sighed, digging into his wallet for a couple of bills.

"Don't worry about it. This one is on me," I said, reaching into mine. I tossed down enough to cover our bill, as well as a generous tip for Jon.

"Thanks for meeting up tonight. I better get home before Hannah has the entire wedding planned without me," he joked. "Or better yet, maybe I should stay out a little while longer?"

I tipped my head back and laughed.

"I would rush home if I were you. She's probably ordering a pink vest and polka-dot bowtie for you as we speak."

His eyes widened with mock surprise.

"Are you heading over to Elena's?"

I picked up my phone and opened the new message from her.

"No," I shook my head. "She said she has a headache and is going to bed. I'll check on her in a little bit to see how she's doing."

"Do you want me to stop by on my way home?" he offered, slipping into his leather jacket.

I hated not knowing if she was okay or not, but even more, I hated the sudden overprotective feeling that was consuming me.

"Yeah, if you don't mind?"

"I'll text you in a bit," he said, clapping my shoulder before he took off.

It was after nine by the time we left, but I was too wound up to go home and wait around to see if she was okay. Instead, I went to work and decided to burn off some energy there.

<u>Six</u>
Elena
10 Days Ago

"No, ma," I groaned into the phone. "I don't need to come stay the night; I'm fine."

"The power is out, and you're by yourself in the dark. Don't be silly, Elena. Just come home, and I'll make you dinner."

My stomach growled at the thought, and I wondered how desperate was I for company and whether a homemade meal was enough to get me over there. It was the middle of the week, and I had already run out of the groceries I had bought on Sunday while I was out with Trevor. Where all of the food went, I had no idea. I didn't remember eating half of what was missing, but the extra curve in my ass suggested that maybe I had.

"I have an early day tomorrow. I'm just going to read a book and then go to bed."

"How are you going to read in the dark?" she countered, calling me out on my lie.

"I have an app on my phone. That's how I read all of my books."

"So you're going to drain the battery on your phone to read

a book? What if there's an emergency, and then you can't call for help because your phone is dead?"

Ugh. She had a point.

"Just come have dinner with us, Leni. I'm making risotto, your favorite."

I looked outside at the dark, cloudy sky. It was cold with the promise of another snowstorm coming soon, but if anything was going to lure me out in this weather, it was my mother's risotto.

"Fine," I grumbled. "I'll be there in thirty minutes."

I hung up and sent a quick message to Trevor, letting him know that I would be at my parent's house for a while. He had been overly anxious lately and suddenly needed to know where I was at all times. I didn't know if it was because of the phone charger incident the other day or if Max was more in his ear now that he knew about us. Either way, I could feel him hovering, and it was spiking my anxiety even further.

There was no need to get ready, but I still made sure to run a comb through my hair and take it out of the messy ponytail it had been in since I got home from work. The last thing that I needed was my mom worrying about whether or not I could handle living on my own and working a full-time job. I knew the circles under my eyes would already concern her; I didn't want to add fuel to the fire by looking too tired to take care of myself.

I pulled on my NYU hoodie and shoved my phone into the pocket before grabbing my backpack and flinging it onto my shoulder. Luckily I had an extra charger that I kept in it so I could make sure to charge my phone at my parent's house just in case the power wasn't restored by the time I got home.

The streets were quieter than usual, likely due to the weather getting worse. I walked quickly, making my way to the subway as I tried to escape the bitter cold. Once I got on the train, I found a seat in the back and sat down. There was an older man across from me, reading a newspaper, and a mother on the other side of the train, peeling back a banana for her toddler. It wasn't overly crowded, yet I felt the uncomfortable feeling of someone watching me.

I tried to shift my focus after I couldn't find the source of the perceived threat I was feeling. The speaker announced the next stop, and I stood up, ready to get off. I held onto the bar above me as I walked down the aisle and waited by the door. The train jerked to a stop, and the doors slid open.

Just as I stepped onto the platform, I felt a heated gaze burning into the side of my head. I turned and looked over my shoulder as the doors pinched shut behind me. Sitting a few seats over from the door was a man wearing a hoodie. He looked up right as the train started to pull forward, and I saw Trevor's unmistakable face.

By the time I got to my parent's house, my blood was boiling. I knew that things between Trevor and I felt a little strained lately, but I couldn't believe that he had sunk to the level of spying on me. Didn't he trust me? I had told him where I was going, so there shouldn't have been a reason to follow me.

I opened the door and walked in, a soft smile pushing across my face at how comfortable it felt to be home, the immediate feeling of being safe and protected. I knew that it would be different to live by myself, but I hadn't expected the level of fear that came along with it. Whether or not that was normal for people living alone for the first time, who knew. I didn't have anyone I could ask without having them immediately judge me and try to talk me out of it. As far as they were concerned, I was still the helpless victim who needed to be protected. And I was tired of it.

Seven
Elena
9 Days Ago

"Okay, so walk me through what happened," Natalie said softly, leaning back in her chair.

I was sitting across from her, my foot tapping anxiously on the imported foreign rug that matched the eclectic décor in her office as I tried to force my thoughts to come out more calmly than what I had felt.

Last night I got a text message back from Trevor while I was at my parent's house, thanking me for letting him know that I had gotten there alright. He claimed that he was stuck at work, trying to put together some marketing material to draw in more clients for the new year. I stared at his message for so long that I thought that my phone would burst into flames from the fire that was roaring inside of me. It was one thing to follow me but another for him to lie about it and act like he didn't see me catch him at the end.

"It's Trevor," I said angrily through gritted teeth. "He followed me last night."

She lowered her head until her glasses slipped down to the end of her nose, and she looked over them to see me. A single eyebrow arched, and I knew that she was as shocked by this information as I had been.

"The power was out in my neighborhood last night, so I decided to go to my parent's house for dinner. I texted Trevor to let him know that I was heading over there so he wouldn't be worried about me since we both know he's been a little overprotective since the charger incident." I paused and forced out a frustrated breath, pressing my feet flat against the floor so I would stop moving. "I kept feeling like someone was watching me on the train. It was this eerie feeling that I couldn't shake. I looked around several times and didn't see anything odd, so I tried to ignore it. When I stepped off of the train, I looked over my shoulder and saw him."

I shook my head as the anger started fueling the fire inside me that I hadn't been able to put out since it happened. When I called to schedule a last-minute appointment with Natalie this morning, she had gone out of her way to squeeze me in on her lunch break. Not that she was actually taking one with the sushi still sitting untouched on her desk, getting dangerously close to going bad.

"What did he do?"

I let out a maniac laugh and instantly regretted it. I was *this* close to feeling like I was about to lose my shit—which was why I was sitting in my therapist's office when I should have been at work.

"He just stared at me. Sat there and acted like it was nothing."

Natalie pushed her glasses back up her face and turned to her computer, typing something before she returned her attention to me.

I glanced at the clock hanging on the wall behind her and knew that we only had ten minutes before her next appointment would be here.

"Have you asked him about it?" she asked, swiveling her chair to face me.

"Nope," I shook my head. "I've been too pissed off to talk to him. He texted me back after I got to my parent's house and thanked me for letting him know I was there. Lied about being stuck at work."

"Did you respond to it?"

"No."

She leaned back in her chair and folded her hands in her lap.

"Why do you think he followed you?"

"I have no idea," I blew out. "I'm tired of everyone hovering over me, worrying that I'm some fragile baby that they have to take care of."

She offered a sympathetic smile but said nothing. We had been doing this long enough that we didn't need to go into those details anymore. She knew how I felt about the constant attention that my family gave me and how I struggled to get past my frustration that they didn't trust me to take care of myself. And maybe it was for a good reason. I had been reckless when Adam took me, and they all knew that. Sure, people make mistakes and learn from them all the time, but mine almost killed me. I guess I could see where they were coming from on some level, but that still didn't make what Trevor did okay.

"I think the best approach would be to sit down with Trevor

and ask him about it. Be upfront and honest. It won't do either of you any favors if you're not."

"What if I can't get past my anger with him?" I asked, worried that I would let it get the best of me and ruin the best thing that had ever happened to me.

"Then you need to let him know that you're angry. It's not your job to shield him from your emotions, Elena. It's your job to share them openly with him. If you feel that he did something wrong, then it's your responsibility to tell him. He may disagree, and he may not understand your feelings, but that's for him to sort through and process—not you."

She spun around to answer her phone, letting her receptionist know that she would be out in a moment.

"Relationships take work, and you owe it to yourself to give this one a chance. If you don't, you'll never know what it might have been. Go home, take a nice bath, and try to relax. When you're feeling calmer, reach out to Trevor and find time to talk to him. In-person, Elena. Not text. Face to face where you can see his emotions, and he can feel yours."

I sighed and stood up, knowing that she was right. I hadn't come here looking for her to fix things between Trevor and me, but I felt better knowing that I had been able to get some of my anger out before I talked to him.

"Thanks for squeezing me in at the last minute," I said, glancing down at her uneaten lunch. "I owe you sushi next time."

"No, you don't," she laughed and picked it up. "I actually didn't bring anything else to eat today and forgot that I had this in the fridge. I was about to eat it when I noticed the expiration date passed a few days ago. I didn't want to interrupt you by leaving to go throw it away."

"Well, I'm glad that you didn't eat bad sushi," I said, scrunching my face in disgust. I unzipped my purse and grabbed a granola bar out of the side pocket. "Here, this isn't lunch, but it'll hopefully hold you over until you can grab some real food."

She smiled and took it, the kindness in her eyes lighting up her face the way it always did.

"Thank you, Elena. I appreciate it."

"See you on Monday," I said nervously, hoping that I could wait that long to see her again. Something about being here and talking to her was calming, which was another thing that I deeply missed these days.

"If you need anything before then, you know how to reach me," she assured me as I walked through the door.

Once I got to my apartment, I went inside and locked the door, making sure both locks were in place. It was an obsessive habit that I had started since I moved in, but lately, it felt like I constantly kept forgetting whether or not I had locked the door. Natalie assured me that stress could cause problems with remembering stuff, which wouldn't be a big deal if it wasn't something as important as making sure the door was locked and that I was safe inside.

Taking her up on her advice, I made my way to the bathroom and started a bath. Soaking in a hot bubble bath sounded wonderful, and the smell of lavender was sure to soothe me. While the tub was filling, I went to grab the book I was reading and my phone, just in case anyone needed me.

I got back to the bathroom and set everything down as

I stripped my clothes off and stepped in. The water was borderline too hot, but once I sat down, the heat started to melt my stress away.

My phone chimed, alerting me to a new text message.

Trevor: Hey, I feel like we haven't seen each other much lately. Can we get together soon and talk?

I was about to text him back and ask why he had been following me when I remembered Natalie's advice— i*n person, Elena. Not text. Face to face where you can see his emotions, and he can feel yours.*

I worked my jaw back and forth in frustration, ready to get past this hiccup and move on. I loved Trevor—even if I hadn't verbally admitted that to him yet—and didn't want this to end over something stupid. Maybe he had a good explanation for why he had been following me?

I fought the urge to open the door to a conversation via text message and simply replied *Okay*.

I put my phone on the edge of the tub and lowered my shoulders into the water as I closed my eyes and tried to remember a time when I didn't feel so overwhelmed and stressed.

<u>Eight</u>
Trevor
9 Days Ago

"Christmas is two weeks away. Have you figured out what you're getting for Elena?" Roman asked as he rounded his desk and sat down, bringing his coffee cup to his lips.

I sighed and tossed my pen onto my desk. It was hopeless. Everything was so frustrating and confusing between us right now that I had no idea what to get her.

"I'm going shopping with Max later. I'm sure I'll find something while we're out," I mumbled, cracking my neck.

"Are you guys fighting?" He eyed me cautiously before turning to his computer to check his email.

"Not fighting. Things are just—I don't know—weird between us."

"How so?"

I blew out a breath and leaned back in my padded rolling office chair, resting my feet on my desk.

"She's so distant with me all of a sudden. Like I did something wrong, but she won't tell me what it is."

He chuckled under his breath and shook his head while he

scanned his inbox.

"So then apologize."

"For what?"

"Whatever you did wrong."

"But I didn't do anything wrong."

"Then she wouldn't have any reason to be mad at you, now would she?"

I narrowed my eyes and stared at him, hoping I would develop some sort of superpower that would drill a light into the side of his head, and I could see what he was really thinking. Roman was a man of few words, but unfortunately, he was usually right.

"So what you're saying is that I should apologize and hope that she gives in and tells me what I did wrong in the first place?"

He pointed a finger at me and winked.

"Bingo. Admit that you know that she's upset with you and that you're sorry for whatever you did, but that you want a chance to talk about it so you can avoid upsetting her in the future."

"And that's supposed to work?" I tried to keep the doubt out of my voice, but it didn't work. Elena was the youngest of seven kids—six girls, with Max being the only boy. She came from a large Italian family that lived in the Bronx. I knew better than to think that I would get off easy if I really did do something to piss her off. I had seen her angry plenty of times watching her grow up, and I've always been thankful that I was never on the receiving end.

"You won't know unless you try, now, will you?" He laughed and pushed away from his desk, letting his chair roll back to the wall. "I've got a new client coming in at eleven, so I'll be up front if you need me."

"Sounds good," I said, offering him a half-assed wave as he left. It reminded me that I needed to start bringing in more clients if we were going to keep the momentum going and finish the year as strong as we had started. I made a quick note to reach out to past clients and talk to them about their goals for the new year. Thankfully, being a personal trainer meant that I saw an increase in business every January with the handful of health and wellness resolutions made.

I picked up my phone and checked for a text from Elena. She was supposed to be at work today but had called in—again—complaining of another headache. I had asked Max about it and if she had a history of chronic headaches or if this was something new. He couldn't remember her having them growing up, so I had been worried that maybe something was making her sick in her new apartment. My mind had been fixated on as many different toxins as possible before Max assured me that she was probably just stressed and needed to rest for a few days.

I sent her a quick text and set my phone down, determined to get some of the billing done that I needed to send out before the end of the month. My attention had been so scattered that I was weeks behind what I needed to have done already. While I could stay late and wrap things up, I found that I was more worried about getting home so I could try to spend some time with Elena—when she was actually in the mood to see me these days.

I thought about what Roman had said and decided it

couldn't hurt to apologize to her, even though I had no idea what I would be apologizing for. I've never known her to be a vindictive person who held a grudge, so this felt odd to me. Elena was the type of woman to get mad and make sure you knew it, then she was over it. She didn't draw things out for the sake of getting attention, yet that's what this felt like—her drawing something out without bothering to let me in on what had happened.

A few hours later, I decided that I had made a decent dent in my workload and checked in with Roman before I left. Elena still hadn't returned my texts, and I didn't want to call her if she wasn't feeling well. However, that didn't stop me from making a quick stop at the store to grab a few things to cheer her up.

With a dozen roses in one hand and a bag full of chocolates in the other, I made my way to her apartment, feeling the giddiness that I usually felt when I came to see her. I waited patiently for the elevator and stepped aside to let an elderly couple off before I walked in and pushed the button. Right as the door was closing, I saw Elena walk past me, smiling as she looked up lovingly at the guy next to her. My eyes scanned them quickly before the door closed, my stomach knotting as I saw her fingers laced between his. The dark hoodie he was wearing covered his face, so I couldn't see who it was, but I suddenly had my answer to why she wasn't returning my texts.

<u>Nine</u>
Elena
8 Days Ago

I curled up next to Trevor and tucked my feet underneath me as we watched some action movie that he had picked. I wasn't in the mood for the fast-paced fight scenes, but they seemed to have him occupied as we watched it in silence. Not that I enjoyed talking during a movie, but it felt like we hardly talked at all these days. If anything, at least it still felt comforting to have him physically next to me.

My thoughts were scattered as my mind wandered from the handful of to-do lists that I had. I still had Christmas shopping that I needed to finish, but thankfully my sister, Adelina, needed to finish hers as well, so we were planning to tackle it together tomorrow. Christmas was still two weeks away, and I had the entire weekend to make a dent in my list.

I was lost in thought about what to get Trevor for Christmas when I felt his hand move up from my knee to my thigh. I turned my head to look at him, recognizing the look in his eyes. The movie hadn't ended yet, but without looking at the TV, I could hear the couple having sex. He licked his lips and shifted next to me, drawing me closer as his finger lifted under my chin to tilt my head back as his lips found mine.

The tension in my body started to evaporate as his hand slid up my thigh and around to my ass, pulling me over to sit on top of him. A moan escaped my lips as I lowered myself on top of him and felt his already hard cock beneath me. He deepened the kiss, grabbing my ass more firmly as if he needed to be inside of me as badly as I wanted him. The nice thing about how new our relationship was, was that it didn't take much to get us in the mood for each other.

I slowly pulled away, breaking the kiss as his brow furrowed in frustration. I chewed my bottom lip playfully as I lifted my shirt up and over my head, revealing a new black lace bra that pushed my breasts up and made them look fuller. I had bought it on a whim the other day with the hope of reigniting the spark that had started to fizzle over the past few days.

I waited for him to comment on it, but either he was super horny and didn't notice, or he simply didn't care. I felt the sting of disappointment as my excitement deflated inside of me.

I blew out a frustrated breath, trying to get out of my head and back in the moment when I felt his hands reach up and slide across my back as his fingers worked the clasp on the back. A few seconds later, the bra was being slid off of my body before his eager mouth quickly covered me in kisses and pulled a hardened nipple into his mouth.

My eyes fluttered close as I ran my fingers through his hair, feeling the ache grow between my legs the harder he sucked. Just when it would start to feel like too much, he would release one and move on to the other, capturing it between his teeth before beginning his delicious torture that was slowly pushing me to the edge.

I reached down and ran my hand along this thick cock, loving that he had worn joggers, so I had easier access. He growled against my chest as I rubbed him harder, desperate to feel him.

"Fuck," he groaned, pulling away and making a popping sound as he released my nipple.

In one quick movement, he grabbed me by my waist and flipped me onto my back at the other end of the couch. I laughed and adjusted the pillow under my head as he watched me while pulling my leggings and panties off. Once I was fully naked, I let my legs fall to the side, giving him the view that I knew he loved.

His eyes immediately focused on the Christmas tree landing strip I had done a few days ago. I smiled as he looked up and locked eyes with me.

"Well, that's festive," he said, his voice thick. "I think it's time we see what's under the tree."

"I think it needs a present or two," I joked, enjoying the light-hearted, flirty change to our evening.

"Well, lucky for you, I'm in a giving mood." He dropped his sweats, taking his briefs with them as his erection sprang free. I watched with hungry eyes as his hand wrapped around it, stroking it up and down as he took the few steps toward me and kneeled in front of the couch. His strong hands gripped my thighs as he scooted me over and leaned forward, swiping his tongue along my slit.

I gasped and closed my eyes, savoring the warmth of his mouth as he parted me with his fingers and continued to lick his way across my folds and up to my clit. One of many things that Trevor did well was getting me off quickly with oral sex. His tongue was as magical as a unicorn and earned him *many* compliments in the first few months when we decided to cross the line of him being my brother's best friend and, therefore, off-limits.

My spine started to tingle as my back arched, my desperation to have him get me off starting to take over. I dug my nails into his shoulders, right on the cusp of a mind-blowing orgasm when he pulled away.

My eyes shot open as I stared at him in disbelief. He leaned back and wiped the corners of his mouth while having the nerve to smile at me like he didn't just rob me of one of the best highs of my life.

"What's wrong?" I asked, trying to force the frustration out of my voice as I popped up on my elbows.

He shrugged and licked his lips as he crawled up onto the couch, hovering over me.

"I wasn't ready to exchange gifts yet," he teased playfully before leaning in to nip the bottom of my ear.

"Trust me," he said softly, "you're gonna come when I'm ready for you to."

Before I had the chance to reply, his mouth was on mine, kissing me tenderly as his hands roamed slowly across my body. I felt the prickle of goosebumps left in his wake. As mad as I was a few minutes ago, that anger was quickly replaced with need as his fingers started rubbing my clit again, bringing me back to where I had been before he stopped. I arched my back and spread my legs as far as I could, allowing him the access he needed.

"Please, Trevor," I begged. "I'm so fucking close."

I felt his muscles tense around me before he reached down and guided his cock to my entrance. I was wet and ready for him, but I still wanted that orgasm. He pulled his fingers away and slid inside, thrusting hard as I stretched around him. Usually, he went slowly since he was so well endowed, but tonight was different.

I cried out as he pushed further, the sensation both wonderful and overwhelming at the same time. Before I had time to adjust to him, I could feel him rocking deeper as his hands roamed my body and up to my face. I opened my eyes, searching his while our bodies synced together, finding the perfect rhythm. I closed my eyes and lifted my hips, meeting him as he pumped faster. I knew that he would be close by the way he was breathing.

His hand curled up as his thumb gently grazed my jaw. I tilted my head back, panicking for a moment when I felt his hand trail down to my neck. It was one of my triggers, and he knew it, so I didn't know why he was suddenly touching me there. My eyes shot open as my body stiffened in response.

"Trevor," I warned, reminding him that I couldn't stand to have anyone's hands around my throat.

Instead of pulling away, his fingers tightened harder around my throat, quickly cutting off my air supply as his other hand worked between my legs and started rubbing my clit. My senses were in overdrive as I fought the anxiety that was creeping up my spine, along with the teasing sensation of a possible orgasm.

The harder he thrust, the quicker the pad of his thumb

worked against my sensitive nub, and the tighter his grip was around my throat. Just when I was sure that I would pass out, I felt the first spasm in my pussy as his hand dropped away from my neck. His finger kept the pressure that I needed as I came undone under his touch, my body bucking as the most intense orgasm ripped through me. A few seconds later, I felt him release inside of me.

My head was spinning over what had just happened. I waited for him to pull out before I scooted up the couch, grabbed the throw blanket from the back, and wrapped it around myself. I watched him with curious eyes as he rolled over and sat on the other side of the couch.

I gently raised my fingers and touched the spots where he had held me, wondering if I was going to have bruises. I couldn't tell if I was more upset that he had done that, to begin with, without talking to me, or if I was more ashamed that I had one of the most incredible orgasms of my life from it.

"I should get going," he said, bending down to collect his pants from the floor.

"It's Friday night," I replied, feeling as stupid as it sounded. "You always spend the night on Friday."

"I know," he huffed as he slid his joggers up his legs. "But I have stuff to do, so I need to go."

Something felt off with him, but I couldn't figure out what. He finished dressing and pulled his cell phone out of his pocket a few minutes before mine vibrated on the table. I picked it up and found a new text message from him.

Trevor: How are you?

My brows pulled together as I read it, wondering if this was his way of trying to talk about what had just happened. My anger started to flare as I set my phone down in my lap, still naked except for the blanket that I pulled tighter around my body.

"Why are you texting me when you're standing right there?" I asked, irritated.

He laughed softly and kept his head down as he continued to do something on his phone.

I rolled my eyes and reached for the remote. The movie had already ended, and since I was now spending the night by myself, I could pick a chick flick instead of the action ones he had insisted that we watched.

A few minutes later, he had his stuff and was out the door. I put my sweats on and curled up on the couch, ready to start a movie, when I heard my phone vibrate again. I unlocked the screen and opened the new message from Trevor.

Trevor: We need to talk. Dinner tomorrow night? I'll cook at my place.

I clicked out of the text without answering it. I felt dizzy from the game he was playing and still wasn't in the mood to deal with it. If he wanted to talk, he could have stayed and done so. It wasn't like we hadn't had tough conversations in the short time we had been together. For whatever reason, something had changed between us, and I wasn't sure what it was. Ever since we came clean to Max that we were dating, he had started to act different, and I wasn't sure that I was a big fan of it. While I understood that it was hard for him to cross that line with his best friend's litter sister, it hadn't seemed to bother him until now. Maybe Max was getting into his head and making him nervous? He had a way of doing that.

I was about to set my phone down so I could start the movie when I noticed a notification icon on the main screen. I clicked it, remembering that the new cameras I had set up earlier were programmed to alert me whenever there was movement. I had totally forgotten to turn them off before Trevor got here, which meant they had been recording the entire time. I opened the app and watched the video that it had saved. I fast-forwarded, my fingers trembling the closer it got to the part where we had sex.

A few minutes later, I stopped pushing the button and let the video play out on the screen. I watched as he hovered over me, his hand snaking around my throat as a look of horror etched onto my face. I wanted to look away, but part of me needed to keep watching. A few seconds later, he was plowing into me as my face contorted into a mix of pleasure and anguish as I climaxed.

I closed the app and set my phone on the table. Maybe the cameras weren't such a good idea after all.

Ten
Trevor
7 Days Ago

"Any word from Elena?" Roman asked as he walked into the office. It wasn't unusual for us to come into the office on the weekend, but we tried to keep it to as minimal as possible. This time of year, it was almost a guarantee that we would be working weekends as we got ready for the rush of new clients that we would be getting in a few weeks after the new year started.

"No," I sighed, leaning back in my chair and tossing a stress ball into the air before catching it. It was almost flat at this point, not having done much for my stress as I squeezed the life out of it.

"When did you talk to her last?"

He pulled out his chair and sat behind his desk as he pushed the mouse across the mousepad to wake his computer up.

"I sent her a text last night asking her to come over for dinner tonight so we could talk."

Roman turned his head slightly and looked at me, one eyebrow quirked.

"A text?"

I shrugged, feeling the weight of the problem as it sat squarely on my shoulders. I rolled them a few times, hoping to release some of the tension.

"It's the only way I get her to talk to me these days. And even that is rare."

"Are you going to ask her about the other guy?" Roman asked, shifting in his chair before he spun around to face me.

"I have to," I laughed. "Right?"

Now it was his turn to shrug.

"Did you guys ever say that you were exclusive?"

I pulled in a deep breath, feeling my chest rise and fall as I slowly let it out.

"I didn't think that we needed to."

He laughed and tried to keep the humor off his face but failed.

"What's so funny about that?" I asked grumpily.

"Don't get so mad," he said lightly. "It's just that you're thirty and dating someone who is nineteen. You can't just automatically assume that Elena is on the same page as you are if you guys haven't discussed it."

I crumpled up a piece of paper and tossed it across the room into the basketball hoop above the trashcan. He was right, I just hated to admit it.

"Either way, we need to talk. About the other guy. About us." I paused for a moment, trying to force down the nausea that had been threatening me all morning. "I'm not sure if she even wants to be with me anymore. Maybe it's just the weight of the stress that she's been under with everything this year or the trauma she's still dealing with from being kidnapped. Something has changed, and I'm determined to figure out what it is, even if it means that we don't stay together."

Roman offered a sympathetic smile before we both got busy with the work that needed to be done. A few hours later, I still hadn't heard from Elena, so I assumed she wasn't interested in coming over for dinner. I got a text from Max, asking if I could swing by for a few to help him with something for the wedding.

I decided to call it a day early, knowing that my mind was too consumed with everything else to be able to concentrate on work. I arrived at Max's apartment an hour later, smiling when I saw Hannah spread out on the floor with an absurd amount of fabric swatches scattered around her.

"Oh good, you're here!" she squealed and got up to hug me. "We need your help."

"Okay," I laughed as I shrugged out of my coat and hung it by the door. "What can I do?"

"You should have run when you had the chance," Max joked and clapped his hand on my shoulder before closing the door and heading to sit down in the living room. His apartment was a decent size for New York City but still small enough to feel overwhelmed by the amount of stuff spread out in the room.

"You said you needed help, so I came," I laughed, shrugging helplessly as I followed Hannah over to the couch.

"We're having trouble picking the color for the groomsmen to wear," Hannah explained as she sat down and picked up a handful of swatches.

"Don't we just match whatever the girls are wearing?"

"That's a possibility," she answered, her brow furrowed. "But Max seems to think that the guys won't want to wear hot-pink vests or ties."

"Well," I laughed, sitting down and picking up a handful of options so I didn't smush them. "I would agree with that. Pink really isn't my color, let alone *hot pink*."

"That's why we need something that will go with it and pull it all together." She leaned back against the cushion and blew a strand of hair out of her face.

"And I'm the best you could find to help with this?" I wrinkled my nose at the same time that I heard a knock on the door.

"Don't worry," she assured me as she hopped up and ran over to the door. "I called for backup!"

She opened the door, and a frantic-looking Elena walked in. My heart started racing as I took her in, the look of panic on her face as she scanned the room around her as if she was looking for something. Or rather *someone.*

"Elena, what's wrong?" I asked, standing up and turning to face her. Her eyes danced wildly as they found mine.

Max jumped up, rushing over to where she was. Soon, we were all hovering around her, waiting for her to answer us and tell us what had happened.

"Nothing," she said nervously. "I'm fine."

"You don't look fine," I replied quickly, earning a glare from her. I bit down on my tongue to keep from saying anything else that would further upset her.

"I am."

I took a few steps back, giving her some space as Hannah helped her out of her jacket and hung it by the door next to mine.

"What's going on, Elena?" Max asked, legs planted firmly with his arms folded across his chest.

"Calm down; you don't have to go into cop mode," she said with an eye roll. "I said that I'm fine."

"Do you want some tea?" Hannah offered, changing the subject and leading Elena into the kitchen by her elbow.

Even though the space was small, and we could still hear and see them, it felt like there was enough privacy for Max and me to have a quick talk without her hearing.

"Do you know what's going on?" he asked quietly, standing beside me as we continued to watch them in the kitchen.

I shook my head, frustrated that, for once, I had no idea what was going on in her life. How had things changed so drastically between us in just a few days?

"Something's got her rattled," Max commented under his breath. "Maybe she'll talk to you later when you guys are by yourselves, without her big brother hanging over her shoulder."

I snorted and then turned my head to look at him.

"I doubt it."

"Why?"

"Because I'm not sure that there's anything for us to talk about anymore."

I could feel my anger starting to build as I balled my hands into fists and then released them.

"What's going on? Did something happen between you guys?"

"I don't have any fucking idea," I breathed out quietly. "She's been mad at me for who knows what, and when I went over to talk to her the other night, I saw her leaving with some other guy."

Max turned his attention back to his sister and narrowed his eyes.

"What the fuck?" he muttered. "That doesn't sound like her."

"Well, it was. I asked her to come over tonight for dinner so we could talk, and she still hasn't responded to me. So, I guess that makes it really clear where we stand."

A few minutes later, the kettle whistled as Hannah got the tea ready for Elena. They joined us in the living room, and Hannah did her best to get everyone focused on the task of finding matching colors for the wedding party. While I tried to be a team player by offering suggestions and putting different swatches together, I was distracted by Elena constantly being on her phone.

By the time we were done, Hannah was beaming, and Max was relieved that he didn't have to look at any more fabric swatches. I pulled on my coat and was getting ready to ask

Elena about dinner when I saw her checking her phone again.

"Thanks for all of your help, you guys," Hannah said as she walked us to the door.

"No problem," Elena said, still looking down at her phone. "I have to go, but I'll talk to you later."

It was unclear who she was talking to since she didn't bother to make eye contact with anyone before she opened the door and bolted out.

"What was that about?" Hannah asked, looking between Max and me.

"I have no fucking clue," I muttered as I leaned in to hug her.

Max gave me a nod as I left, and I knew that it meant he would call me later when Hannah was busy, and we could talk. As I walked out of their apartment and made my way to the subway, I couldn't shake the feeling that something wasn't right.

Eleven
Elena
6 Days Ago

I woke up with a pounding headache that refused to go away by the time I was supposed to head over to my parent's house for Sunday dinner. I had called my mom and explained that I wasn't feeling well, rushing her off of the phone before she peppered me with questions about what was going on. To say that she was overly concerned about me these days would be an understatement. I had more people up my ass than a frequent flyer at a proctologist's office.

I had no idea what time it was as the day dragged on, my head still throbbing with an intensity that made me nauseous and cranky. When a text message from Trevor came through, asking if we could get together to talk, I promptly ignored it and put my phone on Do Not Disturb while I laid down to take a nap. While I doubted that it would get rid of the headache, at least I wouldn't have to be awake and conscious to deal with it.

The dark clouds outside blocked any traces of sunlight from my room, creating a welcoming environment for me to rest. I laid down and pulled the crocheted blanket that my grandma had made me up to my chin, shivering against the cold chill in the room. I had already turned the heater up several times, yet it felt like it was barely sixty degrees. The last thing I needed right now was a heavy electric bill from blasting the heater when I had missed almost a week of work and would have to find a way to make up those hours. Being on my own was already proving to be a lot harder than I had imagined.

My body finally started to relax into the softness of the mattress as sleep threatened to take over. As my eyes fluttered closed, I saw the shadow of someone walk past my bedroom. My heart jumped out of my chest as I flung the blanket off of me and sat up. I tried to listen carefully for sounds of movement but couldn't hear anything past the blood pulsing in my ears.

I stood up on shaky legs and kept my eyes on the door, looking for a sign of the intruder. My hand reached down between my bed and the nightstand, searching for the baseball bat that I always keep next to me. I fumbled around for a few more minutes, frustrated that I couldn't find it. Finally, I gave up, trusting that I could scream loud enough for a neighbor to come help me if needed—not that it had helped any when I screamed the night that Adam took me.

The panic and reminders of that night rushed through me, sending chills up my spine as I walked through the door and down the short hallway to the living room. I desperately wanted to turn around and look behind me to make sure no one was there, but I had seen enough horror movies to know that it was a rookie mistake. Always keep your eyes open and be alert to all of your surroundings.

I stepped into the living room, quickly scanning the space between it and the kitchen. Everything looked the same as

I had left it not that long ago with no signs of anyone else being here but me. I took a few cautious steps toward the kitchen after determining that the curtains were too flat against the wall for anyone to be hiding behind them. My breathing was shallow as if I was too afraid to let on that I was in the room. Or maybe it was just that I was paralyzed by fear and had forgotten how to breathe.

Everything in the room was quiet and calm as I looked around, feeling crazy for thinking I had seen someone. As I let out the breath that I had been holding, I heard the sound of a lock clicking in place as the front door shut.

TEN SECONDS TOO LATE

Twelve

Trevor

6 Days Ago

Sundays were supposed to be my day to relax and unwind before starting a new week, but today I was anything but relaxed. The past few days with Elena had really gotten under my skin and left me questioning everything between us.

I had racked my brain trying to figure out what had gone wrong between us but kept coming up empty. Nothing had seemed to trigger anything serious, yet here we were, possibly at the end of a relationship that had just started.

The only thing that I could link back to when I started noticing the change was that it all began to unravel after we had come clean to Max about our relationship. He seemed cool with it—surprisingly—but that didn't mean that Elena was still fine with everything. I had known her the majority of her life since Max and I became best friends at an early age. I also knew how close she was to her family and how important her brother's opinion was to her.

But was that really enough to drive her away and into the arms of another man? Or was Roman right that she was just young and didn't know how to be in a committed relationship? Better yet, maybe it was the fact that we hadn't sat down and discussed what we wanted from this when it started. I was crazy about her and couldn't imagine being with anyone else, but that didn't mean she was on the same page. Which should have been obvious since I saw her holding hands with someone else a few nights ago.

I shook my head as if to clear the frustration that was forcing its way through my head again. It was like trying to solve a Rubik's cube—impossible unless you were some sort of child genius, which I wasn't.

Bending down, I picked up the stack of laundry I had just finished folding and took it to the bedroom to put it away. I wanted to pick up my phone and call her, but I knew that she would be at her parent's house for family dinner and didn't want to interrupt her time there. Not like she would answer anyway, given that my text from earlier still went unanswered.

I went to the kitchen, pulled out a packaged salad that I had picked up earlier, and pulled the cover off of it. My fork hovered in the air as I tried to force myself to pierce a piece of chicken and enjoy my meal. Instead, I set it down and picked up my phone, shooting off a text message to Max before I could talk myself out of it.

Me: How's Elena tonight?

Before I could set my phone down, I watched the dots bounce across the screen as he replied.

Max: No idea. She didn't show up for dinner.

Me: Why not?

Max: Headache.

Me: Again?

Max: Same thing I said.

I blew out a heavy breath as I scrubbed a hand down my face.

Me: Are you going to check on her?

Max: Heading that way now.

I set my phone down and pushed my salad away from me. I didn't have to ask Max to update me once he knew if she was okay; I knew that he would as soon as he knew. It was the waiting part that was going to kill me.

# TEN SECONDS TOO LATE

Thirteen
Elena
6 Days Ago

My heart was still racing as I whipped open the door and looked down the hall, trying to find whoever had just been in my apartment. The only thing that I saw before the elevator door closed was a dark hoodie that looked a lot like Trevor's. I bent over and tried to catch my breath after running down the hall, the mix of adrenaline and fear pushing my nausea up my throat.

If I thought that my headache was bad before, it was ten times worse now. I stood up and made my way back to my apartment, checking over my shoulder every few steps just to make sure that whoever it was didn't somehow make their way back up to my apartment.

Part of me wanted to be the superhero you see in movies that dashes down the stairs and makes it to the elevator right as the doors slide open, and you see who's inside. I contemplated the idea for half a second until I realized that I would likely die from exertion before I even made it to the second floor. Pasta and heavy carbs had become my lifestyle lately, and the extra pounds they added to my ass would only make it that much harder to run after someone.

I went inside and locked the door, my fingers trembling as I slid the chain into place. I stepped back and stared at it, daring someone to try to come in again.

My breathing was finally starting to return to normal when my phone vibrated across the counter, whipping my attention from the door to it. I rolled my eyes at my reaction, knowing that there was nothing to be afraid of. It was simply a text, and most likely, it was from Trevor.

I picked up my phone and slid my finger across the screen to unlock it.

Max: I'm on my way up. Open the door.

I sighed heavily as I typed out my response.

Me: Have you ever heard of saying please?

Max: Open the door.

I set my phone on the counter and walked to the door, looking through the peephole to make sure he was actually there. Once I saw his head moving from side to side, scanning the area, I slid the chain and then reached down to unlock the door.

"Hey," I said, trying not to sound too breathy. I leaned my arm against the door as casually as I could.

He narrowed his eyes and came inside, his shoulders tense and rigid as he walked around in full cop mode. I waited for him to finish whatever he was looking for so he could get on with why he was there.

"What's going on, Elena?" he asked, running a hand through his hair before turning to look at me.

"Nothing." I shrugged and then wrapped my arms around myself, trying to get warm again.

"Why's it so cold in here?"

"I don't know," I confessed. "I turned the heater up earlier, but it doesn't seem to stay warm, and I can't afford to keep cranking it up right now."

He walked over to the thermostat on the wall and leaned forward to read the tiny numbers.

"It's set to sixty-two, Elena. It needs to be at least sixty-eight for it to stay warm." He reached up and pressed the buttons until he was satisfied with the new temperature. "I'll give you money for the bill."

I rolled my eyes and shook my head.

"Seriously, Elena, you can get sick from keeping your apartment that cold. It's not going to change your electric bill that much to keep it a little warmer in here."

"I know that," I scoffed, frustrated because I knew that there was no way that I had left it at sixty-two.

"Then why do you have it turned down so low?"

"I didn't!" I cried out, my emotions getting the better of me. This was too much—all of it was just too much for me to handle right now.

"Then why was it set that low? Is your heater broken?" He stepped closer to me, putting a hand on my shoulder as I trembled.

"I don't know. It doesn't seem to be."

"So then *you* set it to that temperature?"

I could hear the confusion in his voice.

"No," I snapped, hating that we were about to have this conversation.

"Then who did?"

"The hell if I know! Probably the same person that I caught leaving my apartment a few minutes ago."

He pulled his hand away and immediately reached behind his back for his gun. He didn't actually pull it out, but I could tell that it was a natural reaction for him.

"Someone was in your apartment?"

His eyebrows were raised so high they didn't look like they were still attached to his forehead.

I nodded, unable to say anything more.

"Why didn't you call me? Which way did they go?"

He was standing right in front of me, the smell of garlic fresh on his breath from dinner at my parent's house.

"I saw someone in the elevator as the door closed. I didn't get there in time to see their face or anything else."

"Was it a man? A woman? How tall were they? What were they wearing?"

He was going a mile a minute and sending my blood pressure even further through the roof.

"Seriously, Max—you have to calm down with the whole cop thing. You're going to give me an embolism here in a few if you don't stop rapid-firing questions at me."

I felt the air change around us as he took a step back and

turned around, trying to get it together. I knew this was as hard for him as it was for me, given the whole kidnapping thing last year.

"I will try to stop asking so many questions at one time, but I need you to sit down and walk me through *every single detail* of what happened. It's very important, Elena."

I nodded and followed him over to the couch. The heater kicked on, the sound startling me for a second until I was comforted by the warmth that was floating between us.

"Start from the beginning," he instructed as he sat down across from me and pulled out the notepad and pen that he always kept in his coat pocket.

"I don't even know where to start," I laughed, feeling as crazy as everything was about to sound. "Strange things have been happening for a week or so now, and this just adds to all of that."

"Like what?"

I pulled in a deep breath and slowly let it out. Natalie had taught me to focus on my breathing when I needed to calm myself. It used to work, but now it was getting harder and harder to find any peace.

"Like the phone charger incident. Waking up to find the TV turned on in the middle of the night when I know that I had turned it off. Finding the stove turned on when I get out of the shower." I paused for a moment and inhaled again. Once I was ready, I continued. "Today, I've had a terrible headache—so bad that I can barely stand to be awake. I called mom to let her know that I wasn't coming to dinner, then turned up the heater and went to my room to lay down.

I was freezing, so I curled up with the blanket that Nonna made me and laid down. As I was starting to fall asleep, I saw someone walk past my door. I got up and looked around the apartment, trying to convince myself that I had dreamt it until I was in the kitchen and the front door closed."

Max's knuckles were white from how tight he gripped the pen as he wrote the details down.

"What happened after that?" he asked, his voice softer than I had anticipated.

"I went after them. I looked down the hallway to see if I could find which direction they had gone. Then I heard the elevator ding and rushed off that way. I barely got there as the door was closing. I didn't see anything other than they were wearing a dark hoodie."

I wanted to add a snide comment about how it looked a lot like the one that I had seen Trevor wearing a lot lately, but the last thing that I needed was to fill Max's head with worry that his best friend was messing with his baby sister.

Deep down, I wanted to believe that it *wasn't* Trevor, but the person that I saw did look a lot like him with his build and the way he walked. It wasn't likely, but then again, it wasn't impossible. He had been acting strange lately, so there was no telling what he may or may not do.

Max finished writing, then set his pen and notepad on his thigh and leaned forward, resting his arms on his knees.

"Is there something else going on, Elena? Something that you're not telling me?"

I shook my head and frowned, unsure of what he was trying to insinuate.

"I can't help you if I don't know the truth about what's going on. That means I need to know everything, even the stuff you may feel ashamed to tell me. I'm your big brother, Elena. There's nothing that you could ever do that would make me love you any less or think bad of you. You can trust me."

"I've told you everything, Max. I don't know what it is that you think you know, but if you can just spit it out already, that would be great."

I pulled my legs up under me, still trying to get warm even with the heater blasting around us. One thing was for certain—the damn thing wasn't broken by any means.

He leaned back and sighed, running a hand down the scruff on his jaw.

"I know, Elena."

"Know what?" I lifted my hands in the air, thoroughly confused.

"About the other guy that you've been seeing."

My jaw dropped before I could stop it, the tension behind my eyes starting to build again.

"What the hell are you talking about?"

"Let's not play games, Elena. Trevor saw you with someone else. He's been trying to talk to you about it, but you keep avoiding him and acting distant with him."

My mind was going a mile a minute, trying to piece together the story he had just told me. None of it was true, and why Trevor would tell him such a thing was beyond me. Maybe I wasn't wrong about him after all, and he was making up stories to keep Max from finding out what he was really up to. If that was the case, two could play this game.

"Are you kidding me right now?" I asked, pure disgust attached to every word. "If anyone has been distant, it's been him. Not only that, but he hasn't been himself in so long that I'm not sure I even know who he is anymore."

"That's funny," Max laughed sarcastically. "He said the same thing about you."

"And you believe him?"

"I don't know what to believe because you won't talk to me. You won't tell me what's going on. All I have is what he tells me and that he's worried about you. We all are."

"Why bother talking to you? You guys didn't even believe me about the charger. Why would I tell you anything else? Just so you can turn around and make it look like I'm crazy?"

Max blew out a frustrated breath and looked at me, his eyes softer and his tone more sincere.

"No one thinks that you're crazy. We're just worried about you."

"You keep saying that," I snorted.

"Because it's true."

"Then why is Trevor acting the way he is?" I blurted out, knowing that Max likely had no idea what I was talking about. It wasn't like Trevor was going to talk to him about trying to choke his sister out during sex, even though he knew it was a hard limit for her. Either way, something had changed with him, and I was dying to know what it was.

"Acting worried?" he asked, tilting his head to the side.

"No, not worried." I stopped for a moment to think about how I would describe him instead.

"Distant. Cocky. Inconsiderate." I shrugged my shoulders and added, "Weird."

"I don't know, Elena," he said warily, and I could tell that he didn't want to get into the details of our relationship. "I think you guys definitely need to sit down and talk, though."

"That's the problem—he never wants to talk while he's here. He sends me texts while he's standing right next to me, then leaves and sends me another one to ask me to get together for dinner so we can talk. It's weird, and I just don't have the time or energy for these games."

Max frowned, and I could tell that he knew this didn't sound like Trevor either. Good, at least someone else thought it was odd and not just me.

"I don't know what to say," he sighed, lifting his hips to pull his cell phone out of his pocket. "He's texting me now to see how you're doing. He's been worried about you all night. Maybe take the first step and call him this time? I'm sure it's not easy for him to approach you after seeing you with someone else."

"Yeah, maybe," I said, even though I didn't mean it. I needed to figure out what was going on with Trevor and find out why he was making up these stories before I fought with Max about it.

"Well, I need to get back to mom's to pick up Hannah. Are you going to be alright?"

I nodded and pushed up off of the couch to walk him out.

"Be sure to keep that baseball bat by the door, just in case you need it," he said over his shoulder to me.

"I would if I could find it," I muttered, rubbing a hand along the band of tense muscles in my neck.

"You mean that one?" Max asked, nodding to the kitchen counter where it was lying next to a stack of mail that hadn't been there earlier.

My heart dropped as I stared at it, wondering when it was put there. Obviously, sometime before the intruder ran out of my apartment, but it was more jarring not knowing how long they had been there, to begin with, especially since I was home all day and apparently not alone.

"Oh yeah," I said dismissively as I shook my head. "I forgot that I put it there earlier."

Max gave me one final look-over before opening the door and stepping into the hallway.

"Keep the door locked and call me if you need anything. I can be here in a few minutes."

"Will do," I said as I forced a smile and closed it behind him.

I quickly locked both locks and slid the coffee table over to block the door, just for good measure. Then I walked over to the counter and moved the baseball bat to the side as I looked at the stack of mail that had been sitting underneath it. As I picked it up and sorted through it, a picture fell to the floor. I bent down and picked it up, wondering who the beautiful girl was with so much sadness in her eyes.

Fourteen
Trevor
5 Days Ago

I tapped my fingers anxiously on the table, rattling my coffee cup as I waited for Max to show up. He had sent a quick text last night that said that Elena was fine and that we should talk in the morning. We decided to meet at the café on the corner, but he had yet to show up.

I glanced down at my watch, checking the time as the seconds ticked by. The waitress glanced in my direction, looking to see if I was ready to order. I shook my head no and continued to stare out the window, waiting for him to get there.

Obviously, Elena was safe—otherwise, Max wouldn't have left her apartment last night. The part that got me and had me up in arms was that he wanted to talk to me. I didn't know if it was the tone of his text—was that even a thing? This morning it definitely felt like a thing. Or if it felt like the dreaded, *we need to talk* conversation that everyone hated in relationships. As much as I had been trying to push the thought out of my head all night and this morning, I couldn't help but wonder if Elena had sent Max here to break up with me.

Ten minutes later, I felt like my heart was going to explode out of my chest. Thankfully, Max showed up at that moment, and the look on his face looked like he was about to put me out of my misery.

I leaned back against the worn-out booth and blew out a breath. *Here it comes.*

"Hey," Max said as he slid out of his jacket and into the booth opposite of me. "Sorry I'm late. Hannah wasn't feeling well this morning."

"Is she okay?" I asked, my voice scratchier than I expected. I sipped my coffee, hoping that it would help.

"I hope so." He tossed his gloves on the table and then set his phone down, checking for any new notifications. "She's not sure if she caught a stomach bug or if she has food poisoning, but she's been throwing up since last night."

"That sucks," I mumbled, too distracted by what he was going to say about Elena to be able to focus on anything else right now.

"Yeah, her mom is coming to stay with us in a few days, so I hope she's better by then."

I nodded and looked around, counting down the seconds until my life would explode around me. Okay—so maybe that was a little dramatic, but the thought of losing Elena pulled at my heart in a way that I had never felt before, and I honestly wasn't sure that I would survive losing her.

"Anyway, the reason why I asked you to meet me this morning..." he started, his voice tapering off as the waitress walked by.

"Thank fuck," I mumbled, relieved that he was finally going to get to it. I felt my jaw tense when the waitress turned around and noticed him sitting there, choosing that moment to take our order.

A few painstakingly long minutes later, I ordered food I had no plans of eating and leaned forward to make sure I heard every word out of Max's mouth.

"Alright, where was I?" he asked, looking as frazzled as I felt.

"Elena," I blurted out impatiently. "If you're here to break up with me for her, please just do it already and put me out of my misery."

Max let his head fall back as a laugh tumbled out of his mouth.

"You're kidding me, right?" he joked, the corners of his lips still tugging up as he tried to be serious.

I pinned him with a look as I locked my hands together in front of me on the table.

"She didn't send me here to break up with you," he confirmed with an eye roll. "And even if she did, I would have said no and made you two work your own shit out."

"Good to know," I mumbled, feeling somewhat relieved.

"I'm here because I'm worried about her. When I went to check on her, she was panicked and said that someone had been in her apartment."

My heart chose that moment to explode out of my chest as I stared dumbly at him, unable to speak.

"What the fuck?" I finally asked, trying to get my thoughts together. "Why didn't you tell me last night? I could have gone over there and stayed with her. Or had her stay with me. Did you check her apartment? Have any leads on who it was or what they wanted?"

My mind was going a mile a minute, the questions spewing out faster than fireworks on the Fourth of July.

"Calm down," Max said sternly, looking around to make sure I hadn't drawn attention to us. "*That's* why I wanted to talk to you in person. I didn't want you freaking out and rushing over to her apartment and making things worse."

"Worse?" My eyebrows shot up my forehead. "How would I make it worse?"

"By doing what you're doing right now. I know that you love her and that you want to protect her, but you can't freak out every time something happens to her."

"And why the fuck not?"

"Because she needs us to back off and let her live her life without keeping her in a bubble. She has to be able to experience things—the good and the bad—without us constantly intervening and rescuing her before she has a chance to figure it out herself."

"You're starting to sound like Elena," I muttered, trying to force my shoulders to relax a bit.

"That's because those are her words—not mine. Trust me; there's nothing that I would love more than to wrap her in a bubble and protect her from this ugly world that we live in, but it's not fair to her. She deserves to have a life and not constantly live in fear after what Adam did to her."

"But someone broke into her apartment. How are you not upset and freaked out about that?"

Max leaned back as the waitress slid his plate in front of him. Once she was gone, he picked up his fork and studied his plate before answering.

"I was. When I first got there and she told me that she had seen someone in her apartment—it took everything that I had in me not to throw her over my shoulder and lock her in my apartment, so I could watch over her. I yelled at her—which I instantly felt bad about—for not calling me the second that it happened, but then when she explained everything, I realized that she did everything that I would have told her to do if she had called me."

"So what now? We just let someone sneak around her apartment and do nothing?" I questioned.

"I couldn't find any evidence that anyone had been there. I checked the doors and windows, no signs of forced entry. So unless someone had a key, I don't know how they would have gotten in. She said that she was starting to fall asleep when she saw them, that it woke her up, and she went looking for them."

"Did she at least take a weapon with her?"

"She couldn't find the baseball bat that she keeps by her bed. She said that she went through the living room and kitchen and didn't see anything that looked out of place, but then she heard the door close, and that's when she followed them into the hallway."

I pushed a breath of air out as steadily as I could, the tension in my shoulders starting to build again.

"Someone was getting into the elevator as she caught up with them, but she couldn't see who it was."

"Do you think that she made it up?" I asked, hating the doubt in my voice.

He shook his head and took a bite of his eggs. After he finished chewing, he wiped his mouth and said, "No, I don't think that she made it up. But, I do think that the lack of sleep and stress that she's been under might have made her think that she saw something that she didn't."

"So you're not worried that there's an actual threat to her," I said slowly, starting to put everything together. "You're worried that she's about to have the breakdown that we've all been trying to avoid."

He nodded and pushed his plate to the side before setting his fork on top.

"She's going to fall, and she's going to fall hard. I need you there to catch her before she hits rock bottom."

I scrubbed a hand down my face, feeling the weight of what he was asking me to do.

Fifteen
Elena
5 Days Ago

I sat outside the door to Natalie's office, waiting for her to come in. Usually, her receptionist was here to let the clients in, but it seemed no one was running on time this morning. Guess that was a Monday morning for you.

I hadn't slept last night and spent the majority of the night staring at the door in my bedroom, waiting to see someone walk by again. Finally, around three in the morning, I gave up and went to lay on the couch, convinced that I would sleep better out there. Instead, I heard the sirens and sounds of the city, which were a reminder that there was crime happening all around me and that I would likely never feel safe again.

My phone said it was 8:25, which meant that Natalie was almost half an hour late for our meeting. I chewed the inside of my cheek nervously, wondering if she had stood me up or worse—if something had happened to her. I was about to stand up and leave when I heard heels clicking on the tile floor in the hallway that leads to her office.

She rounded the corner with her head down, her fingers flying rapidly across her phone. Before I could say anything to let her know that I was there, she looked up and jumped, bringing her hand to her chest as her phone went flying to the floor next to me.

"Elena!" she exclaimed, her eyes still wide with surprise. "What are you doing here?"

I stood up and dusted off my pants, pulling my brows together in confusion. I grabbed her phone and handed it to her.

"I'm here for my appointment?"

Now it was her turn to look confused.

"But it's not until this afternoon." She unlocked her phone and pulled up her calendar to confirm. "See," she said, turning it toward me. "Your appointment is today at 4:30."

I leaned in and looked at the screen, seeing my name in bold, right at the bottom as the last appointment of the day.

"You changed my appointment?" I asked, feeling stupid for showing up early. Had they called and confirmed that it was going to change?

"No," she said softly. "You changed it two weeks ago and asked for an afternoon spot instead of morning, so you didn't have to miss work."

"I did?"

She nodded and regarded me cautiously as she waited for the pieces to fall into place in my head. Unfortunately, they didn't.

"I don't remember doing that," I muttered. "Sorry, I'll leave and come back this afternoon."

Natalie reached into her purse and pulled out her keys. After unlocking the office door, she stepped to the side and waited for me to go in.

"You don't have to see me right now," I said, feeling bad for derailing her day.

"I don't have an appointment until ten this morning."

"Is that why Abby isn't here yet?"

"Yeah, she wasn't feeling well, so I told her to come in later if she felt like it. It's a slow day for me today, so I can manage on my own if she's not better."

I took a deep breath and looked around the small waiting room that I had sat in a few times a week for the past year. I had always found it calming, and it was one of the reasons that I hadn't turned and ran in the opposite direction the moment I first agreed to come. Max had insisted that I do a handful of sessions before I could give up, and after I met Natalie, I decided that I wasn't ready to stop.

"Are you going in late to work today?" Natalie asked, pulling me out of my thoughts. She unlocked her office door, and I followed her inside.

I chewed my lip nervously before answering.

"I actually called in."

Her head whipped up in surprise. She tried to keep her expression neutral—it was what she did best as a therapist, but even I saw the concern on her face.

As quickly as it appeared, it disappeared, and she pulled her shoulders back and sat down in her chair. I sat where I always sat and crossed my legs, hoping to shield myself from her judgment somehow.

"You seem to be missing a lot of work these days," she noted. "Are they okay with that?"

"I'm not sure," I admitted. "They haven't said anything so far, but I doubt that they're considering giving me a promotion or raise any time soon."

"Do you want to talk about work?" she asked, turning on her computer and moving her mouse around once the monitor lit up.

"Not really," I laughed, still feeling nervous.

"How about some coffee or tea?" she offered, pushing away from her desk. She walked over to the station that she had set up in the corner of the room.

"Tea would be great," I said. "Decaf if you have it."

She nodded and inserted the k-cup into the Keurig before turning and studying me as she leaned against the wall and waited for it to brew.

"You look tired," she said passively as if making a general note to add to her files after I left.

"I am," I laughed, too tired to try to hide it.

"Still not sleeping well?"

"I had another *incident*," I said, my voice dropping on the last word.

She turned to finish the tea and inserted another k-cup into the machine as she started her coffee in the travel mug that she had brought with her.

"What happened?" she asked over her shoulder as she added honey and stirred.

This wasn't the first time we'd chatted over tea, so it wasn't any surprise that she remembered how I liked it.

"I saw someone in my apartment."

She whipped around, knocking over the bottle of honey in the process.

"Are you okay? Did you call the police?" Her voice rose an octave with her concern.

"I didn't have time to. By the time I followed them to the elevator and went back inside, Max was already on his way up to my apartment."

"Did he know that someone had been there?" she asked, brows furrowed as she handed me the cup of tea. I carefully took it from her and set it on the coaster by the edge of her desk.

"No, he was just coming by on his own. I told him about it, though."

"What did he say?"

She finished stirring the sugar and creamer into her coffee, put the lid on, and joined me at the desk again. I went over everything that had happened—the missing baseball bat, the door closing as someone left, and the fact that my *detective* brother hadn't seemed concerned that anything strange had happened since there were no signs of anyone breaking and entering. She nodded and took notes but didn't have much to say about any of it, which made me feel even more uneasy. *Why was no one worried about this?*

"Did you get a chance to talk to Trevor?" she asked casually as she finished jotting something down on her notepad. She looked up and waited for my answer.

I swallowed hard, trying to decide whether or not I wanted to tell her what had happened.

"I um, tried to," I said nervously.

"What happened?"

"He texted me on Thursday and asked if we could get together to talk. I remembered what you said about talking to him in person, so I was short with my text back and said, *okay*. He came over Friday, but he was acting different, and I just assumed that he was mad at me for being short with him, or maybe he was acting that way because he knew that I had caught him following me on the subway. I don't know."

I paused and looked away, remembering the way his hand had felt around my throat. I could feel myself beginning to panic again as my breathing increased and my heart started racing.

"Elena, it's okay to talk to me. This is your safe space," Natalie said calmly. "Take a few deep breaths if you need to, and then try to tell me what happened that's bothering you."

I did as she suggested, pulling deep lungfuls of air in and slowly releasing them back out. She knew my triggers and could tell that something had happened.

Once I felt calmer, I told her about him choking me during sex and felt the blush creep up my neck as I admitted that I had an orgasm from it. I knew that people talked to her about all sorts of things, but I couldn't imagine their sex lives were part of it. Surprisingly she remained unaffected and didn't seem bothered in the least as she talked to me about how this is a kink for many people and that the decreased oxygen can make an orgasm more intense. Even though I didn't feel better about Trevor doing it, I did feel better that I had told someone else, and they hadn't judged me for it.

"When it happened, how did you feel?" she asked before clarifying, "with Trevor—did you feel safe? Did you feel like you could trust him?"

I sat back in the chair and thought about it for a moment. My spine tingled the same way it had that night when he first got there, and I realized that I had my answer. I hadn't felt safe with him that night, and that was a huge red flag for me now that I was aware of it.

TEN SECONDS TOO LATE

Sixteen
Trevor
4 Days Ago

"Alright, one more set, and then we're done," I said as I watched my new client raise the bar above her head, her arms trembling slightly with the weight of it. I kept my eye on her, my stance ready to move if she needed help.

A few minutes later, she was finished, and I was done for the day. I cleaned up and made my way back to the office, finding Roman sitting at his desk with a frown on his face as he stared at his computer.

"What's wrong?" I asked, tossing my phone on my desk as I grabbed my bottle of water to refill it.

"These numbers aren't adding up. With all of the new clients that we've been booking, we should have more coming in next month than what it's showing."

I frowned and walked over to stand behind him as I stood over his shoulder and looked at the spreadsheet he was studying.

"That doesn't make sense," I muttered, running a hand down my face. I had spent hours the past few nights trying to get everything updated to get caught up before the end of the year.

"Did you forget to add the sign-ups from last week's promotion?" he asked, looking over his shoulder at me.

"No, they should all be in there. Everything should be there," I said frustratedly.

"Well, something has to be missing."

"Nothing is missing!" I yelled, my voice rattling off the walls as Roman pulled back and looked at me.

I stepped away and pushed a hand through my hair.

"What's going on?" Max asked as he walked into the room, looking between Roman and me.

"Nothing," I bit out, still feeling the anger and irritation building inside of me.

He looked from me to Roman, waiting for him to answer.

"I said it was nothing," I snarled, walking to my desk and slamming the water bottle down.

"It doesn't look like nothing," Max said evenly, shoving his hands into his pockets.

"Whatever," I muttered, swiping my phone from the desk and pushing past him as I walked out.

"I thought we were going to grab dinner?" he called out as I left.

I knew that I owed him more of an explanation, but right now, I couldn't find one to give him. My head was a mess because of everything with Elena, and I knew that deep down, if the spreadsheet was wrong, then that meant that I had done something to screw it up. The last thing that I needed right now was more work on top of what I already needed to finish.

It was after six on Tuesday, and there were only nine days left until Christmas, which meant that I needed to finish my shopping. I had been putting it off, distracted with everything else, and putting in more hours at work than I had ever had to do before. It felt like no matter how hard I tried to get caught up, nothing worked.

I stopped by a food cart, grabbed a quick bite, and then made my way to the store. Not that I had planned on going to the shop where Elena worked, yet I somehow found myself there, wandering the aisles as I hoped that I might run into her.

I had a basket filled with bubble bath and soaking products that I had no idea if my mom would like, but it wasn't like I pictured Roman or Max while shopping for this stuff. I had to make it look like I was there for a reason—without looking like a desperate stalker trying to find time to see my girlfriend and make sure that she was okay.

Plus, I still needed to buy for my mom, and last I knew, she was into this girly stuff. I picked up a lavender ball-looking thing and brought it to my nose as my eyes scanned the store, hoping to catch sight of her. I was still walking with it pressed to my nose as I rounded the corner and ran right into her.

A pile of stuff went flying into the air and fell to the floor around us as she whipped around and looked at me. Her dark hair was pulled tight into a bun on top of her head, showing off the necklace I had bought her last month for her birthday. It warmed my heart to see her wearing it, especially given how hard things had been between us lately.

"I'm so sorry," I said as I tossed the ball into my basket

before setting it down to help her clean up the mess. She bent down, her jeans pulling tight across her ass as she did, and scooped a handful of packets together before setting them on the shelf beside her.

"What are you doing here?" she asked, not bothering to look up at me as we continued to find the ones that had flown further away. I grabbed the few that I had spotted a couple of feet away and handed them to her.

"I needed to finish up some Christmas shopping," I said, reaching down to pick up my basket.

She leaned forward and looked inside, eyeing the contents before looking back up at me.

"Max is more of a citrus kind of guy," she replied, the corners of her lips tugging up slightly at her joke.

"I was thinking about some of this for my mom," I laughed.

She furrowed her brow and reached inside, moving things around to get a better look.

"Your mom doesn't have a tub, so it's going to be hard for her to use some of that."

I swallowed hard and tried to look away before the blush crept up my neck and covered my face.

"Honestly, I have no idea what half of this stuff is. But I'm super behind on finishing my shopping, and this seemed like a good idea before I started."

She smiled, and for the first time in what felt like forever, it felt natural.

"Here, let me see your basket." She extended her hand and

waited for me to pass it to her. Once she had it situated on the shelf beside her, she pulled some stuff out and left the other in the basket. "There, that should work better. I have a couple of new face masks that I was just putting out—before someone scared the shit out of me—that she would probably like as well."

I nodded toward the basket and winked as I replied, "you're the expert, whatever you think she'll like."

A satisfied grin pulled tight across her face as she added a few of the packets to the cart and grabbed the other stuff that she had pulled out.

"I can put those things back," I offered, not wanting to make more work for her.

"It's okay; it's my job."

I followed her through the aisles as she put everything back where it went, and I tagged along like some lost, lonely puppy.

"I'm surprised to see you are working so late," I said, trying to keep the conversation going.

She looked over her shoulder at me with an expression that I couldn't quite read.

"I'm actually working a double shift today. I've missed a lot of work and needed to make up some of my hours, so I can afford to pay rent."

"I can help if you need it," I offered, a little too eagerly.

"Thank you, but no." She turned and faced me, her shoulders squared the way she gets when she's feeling defensive.

"I don't mind," I added more softly.

"I know, and I appreciate it. But I have to learn how to do these things on my own. I can't constantly have everyone saving me all the time. I missed a few days of work, and now I need to make up those hours. My boss was pretty flexible and let me use some of my sick time as well, so that should help."

I avoided saying what I wanted to say and went with, "That's great; it sounds like you've really got a hold on what you need to do."

Inside I was screaming, begging for her to let me help. Before she moved out and got her own apartment, I had offered for her to live with me. It wasn't that we didn't think we would end up living together at some point in the future; Elena had said no because she wanted to know that she could do it on her own first. I knew this was important to her, and I owed her the respect to support her as she did it.

"Yeah, I'm tired, but soon I'll be caught up on my hours and back to my regular schedule. Thankfully we're busy with the holidays, so they were able to let me squeeze in the extra hours."

"Sounds like everything is working out favorably for you." I felt awkward, not knowing what else to say. This was the most I had gotten to talk to her in days—weeks? Who knew at this point. It felt like the days were melting together, and I had no idea what was happening anymore.

"I get off at seven," she said, looking up at me under her dark lashes as she reached over and fixed the bottles of nail polish on the rack. "Do you want to grab a bite to eat?"

My heart started racing the way it used to when we first started dating.

"I would love to."

"Perfect," she smiled. "I need to get back up front and finish unloading the last few boxes of stock that came in. I'll meet you by the door at seven, and if you still need ideas for what to get me, there's this new apple-pear line that came in that is *to die for*. Megan is working that section right now and can help you pick out some stuff ... you know, just in case you need it."

She winked and walked off, tossing me a flirty smile over her shoulder as she disappeared out of sight. I went in search of Megan and found the items that Elena had mentioned. While Megan had suggested a few things that could be used together, I decided to buy the entire collection, as well as the plum-apricot one that she said Elena had been in love with as well.

A couple of hundred dollars later, I stood by the door with bags full of presents as I waited for Elena. People bustled past me as they came in from the bitter cold, ready to get some shopping of their own done before they moved on to the next store. That's what Christmas in the city was like—mindless wandering from store to store until your wallet was empty, your arms were sore from the weight of the bags, and your head felt like it would explode from the overstimulation.

Right at 7:02, I felt Elena walk up beside me as I tucked my phone into my pocket and reached out to hug her. It felt weird like I wasn't sure if this was something that we did anymore. When she didn't pull away, and I felt her body relax against mine, I held her a little tighter and felt thankful that maybe—just maybe—things were starting to get back to normal between us. Max warned me that Elena was spiraling toward a nervous breakdown, but the woman standing next to me looked like she didn't have a care in the world.

Seventeen
Elena
4 Days Ago

I leaned back into the recliner and watched as Trevor moved about in the kitchen, getting the paper plates and napkins before bringing the pizza into the living room. It felt good to be in his apartment again, and I was already feeling like myself again with him.

When he showed up at my work, I was surprised and didn't know how I would feel about it. Things had been so off with us lately, and I was still struggling to find a way to talk to him about what had happened Friday night. It seemed like every time I tried to start a conversation with him, he would start talking about something else or avoid me.

"Are you ready to eat?" he asked as he balanced everything and then set it down on the coffee table.

I scooted off of the chair and slid down to the floor, rubbing my hands together as I waited for him to open the lid to the pizza box.

"I am sooo ready," I said, drooling as the rich aroma filled the room. I reached in and pulled out a slice before scooting over and leaning against the couch while Trevor fixed his plate.

The pizza was delicious—just like it always was— but tonight it tasted better than ever. Maybe I was just overly hungry, but it felt like there was this insatiable appetite inside of me that could devour the whole damn thing by the time Trevor took his first bite.

My stomach growled as I chewed and swallowed, desperate for more. I didn't bother trying to make small talk—there was time for that later. Right now, it was pizza time.

I finished my slice and licked my fingers, not wanting to waste it by wiping it off on a napkin. I reached in and pulled another piece free, looking sheepishly at Trevor before retreating to my spot on the floor, where I huddled against the couch and went back to eating.

Trevor chuckled and leaned back against the other couch, sitting opposite me on the floor. He took a bite and then wiped his face with the napkin while he chewed.

"What's so funny?" I asked between bites.

"Nothing," he laughed. "I just forgot how cute you are when you're hungry."

I smiled and then leaned forward, watching him as I grabbed another slice. I knew that I would probably regret eating this much later, but right now, it felt like what my body needed– Trevor and heavy tomato sauce-covered carbs.

"I was starving," I giggled, finally covering my mouth with the napkin while I talked. I might not have wanted to waste any food by wiping it away, but I was still a lady. Well, sort of.

"Well, there's plenty, so eat up."

I smiled and finished my slice, debating whether or not to

have another. After Trevor finished his and grabbed one more, I felt my stomach start to protest and knew that I was done. I climbed up onto the couch and pulled the blanket hanging over the back of it over me. I felt more comfortable in his apartment than I did anywhere else. Sometimes I kicked myself for being stubborn and not considering moving in with him instead of getting my own place. Sure it's good to be on your own and know that you can do it, but I wasn't sure that the loneliness and discomfort were really anything to brag about.

After Trevor finished eating, he took the box and our trash to the kitchen, then came back and joined me on the couch. I sat up and waited for him to get comfortable before I laid down again, resting my head on his lap. He turned the TV on and flipped through the channels until he gave up and settled on some cooking show.

Neither of us was really into it, but I rolled onto my side and pretended to watch it while I tried to think about how to start the conversation with him that we needed to have. The longer I waited, the more it felt like maybe we would be okay if I didn't bother. Perhaps it was just a little misunderstanding? Both of us had been stressed and overwhelmed with things lately, so it was possible that we just had a couple of off days.

I smiled as I felt his fingers run lightly up and down my side, the way he always did when we cuddled like this together. His touch was always soft and gentle, teasing me with the things that I knew he could do with those fingers. I shifted again, this time making my boobs pop up more in the new bra that I was wearing—the one he didn't seem to notice the other night. I brought my leg forward and twisted my back some, giving him a better view of my ass as his hand slid down and palmed it.

I let out a small gasp as his fingers slid down the crack of my ass and toward the ache that was beginning to build. It had only been a few days, but I already needed him again, my body humming with anticipation of what was about to come.

I rolled onto my back, allowing his hand to move with me as it trailed across my hip and then lingered over my pussy. I looked up at him and chewed my bottom lip. He shifted beneath me, and I could tell that he was getting as worked up as I was.

He locked eyes with me as he flicked the button on my jeans open and pulled the zipper down. I wiggled my hips, allowing him to move them down my body before he tossed them to the floor. He repositioned his hand and pushed the lace of my g-string panties to the side as his fingers slid over my slit.

I opened my legs wider, allowing him more access as I closed my eyes and covered his hand with mine. I needed him inside of me, touching me and teasing me until I came apart. He slowly trailed his finger over my skin, leaving goosebumps in its wake as he delayed my pleasure. I waited a few seconds for him to get to it, but when he didn't, I bumped his hand out of the way and replaced it with my own.

I heard him exhale heavily as he pulled my panties down further, exposing myself to him even more. I dipped a finger inside and moaned before I rubbed it up and along my clit. I knew he was watching me masturbate, even with my eyes closed, but I didn't care. I wanted to get off, and knowing that he was watching, turned me on more than I would have thought.

Wanting to give him a show, I pulled my hand out and then reached down and removed my panties, tossing them to the floor with my pants. Next, I reached up and pulled my shirt up and over my head, adding it to the pile on the floor. I laid back down on his lap, licking my lips as I watched his eyes follow my hand back to my pussy.

My fingers trailed along the Christmas tree landing strip, remembering how much he liked it last time before they were eagerly making their way inside again. I rubbed my clit hard and fast, watching him as I worked myself over. A few seconds later, my hips were bucking off of the couch as my orgasm ripped through me.

Once I was done, Trevor gently nudged me to sit up. When I did, he stood and stripped down, tossing his clothes to the floor with mine. I watched as his dick sprung free, his erection long and hard as it touched his stomach. He gripped it with one hand and slowly stroked it as I watched.

"That's mine," I said, my voice raspy and filled with desire.

I laid down where I had been before and pulled him down to me, so he had no choice but to lay on top of me as his cock slid into my mouth and down my throat. I opened my legs, giving him a place to rest when I felt his tongue lick my slit. I moaned, still sensitive from the orgasm I had a few minutes ago.

I hollowed out my cheeks as I sucked, taking him deeper as I stroked what didn't fit in my mouth with my hand. His tongue was busy licking up my juices as he mercilessly sucked my clit and built me up for another mind-blowing orgasm.

The closer I got, the harder and faster I sucked. I knew that he was close too, but at the last minute, he pulled out. Before I could object, I felt his mouth tight against my pussy as he flicked his tongue rapidly against my sensitive nub, forcing me to climax. I came on his face, my thighs shaking as they tightened around his head.

He laughed and pulled away, gently wiping his mouth as his hard as a rock dick teased me.

"You should have come in my mouth," I said, reaching for him to finish him off.

"I wanted to come in your pussy instead," he whispered, getting up to pick up his pants from the floor.

I knew that he was getting a condom, and as much as I loved that we were safe with each other, I wanted him here and now. I was on the pill, and it wasn't like we hadn't skipped using one the last time we did this.

"We don't need it," I said breathlessly, grabbing his hand and pulling him back to the couch. He raised a brow but sat down and watched as I slid on top of him.

I closed my eyes and moaned as he filled me, stretching me with his thick cock.

"I like the new bra," he said as he reached behind me to unclasp it.

"Thanks," I breathed, not bothering to tell him he had seen it last time.

He flung it across the room and leaned forward, pulling a

hardened nipple into his mouth while he gently pinched the other one between his fingers. I rode him harder, grinding my pelvis against his and squeezing as tight as I could with each thrust.

The harder he sucked my nipples, the more I felt the ache building inside again. This would definitely set a new record with the number of orgasms I had in one day. I wasn't sure if someone could die from too many orgasms, but I was about to find out.

I felt him drop his hands and grab my hips, guiding me as I rode him the way he needed me to. I closed my eyes and kept the rhythm as I felt him come inside me.

His hands released their grip and gently wrapped around my waist, pulling me into him as he held me. And just like that, it felt like we were back to where we had once started.

TEN SECONDS TOO LATE

Eighteen
Elena
3 Days Ago

I headed home from the coffee shop, my legs wobbly and shaky as I pulled my coat tighter around me to fend off the bitter cold. It was late, and I knew better than to meet someone that I didn't know by myself, but I had been mad at my mom and wanted to prove a point.

I tried to stay upright and not fall to the ground the way my body wanted to. I still had such a long way to go, I couldn't give up now. But something was wrong. Something was very, very wrong. I could feel it in my bones, or rather from the numbness that was slowly creeping over my body and forcing me into a deep sleep that I didn't want.

My eyes fluttered shut, the heaviness of whatever was running through my blood too strong to fight. If this was death, it wasn't as bad as I thought it would be.

I could hear faint footsteps walking around me, someone muttering close by but not close enough for me to hear what they were saying. I tried desperately to wake up, to open my eyes and see where I was.

I knew that I wasn't safe—I was very far from safety. I could feel it in my bones. But there was also nothing that I could do about it. I was paralyzed and frozen in this hell, unable to protect myself or fend off the grabby hands that kept reaching out to touch me.

Finally, the room went silent, and the footsteps stopped. I didn't want to allow myself to rest, but my body needed it. I felt weak and knew that I needed my full strength before I tried to do anything to get myself out of this situation.

I laid there—wherever it was—for what felt like forever before my eyes slowly opened, and I took a look around. It was hard to see where I was because it was so dark. The room was cold and empty. Nothing but concrete around me. The walls. The floors. Everything was concrete.

I sat up and felt around in my pockets as I continued to look around for anyone who might be there with me. I found my phone and quickly found my brother's name. I waited nervously, chewing my nails as I looked around.

I was about to give up when he finally answered the phone.

"Hey, Leni," he answered, my heart skipping a beat, knowing that he would come find me now that I had him on the phone. I was still weak and unsure of whether I was alone or not.

"Help me," I whispered.

"What's wrong?" he asked, the concern registering in his voice.

I couldn't answer–my voice was stuck in my throat. A noise off in the distance had caught my attention and made me fearful that someone was there with me and would hear me before I could tell Max to come get me.

"Leni, where are you?" he pressed.

"I don't know. It's dark. And cold." I kept my voice low as I continued to scan the area around me for any signs of movement.

"Try to look around and see if anything looks familiar or if you see anything that you can tell me about."

I looked around, hoping to find something helpful. There was nothing. I knew that I had to give him more information than that, but I had nothing to give him.

"Who's there with you?" he asked.

"I think I'm by myself now," I said shakily. "I'm scared, Max."

"It's gonna be okay," he assured me. "We're gonna work through this together."

I waited patiently for him to tell me what to do. If anyone could save me, it was my big brother.

"Are you able to walk around?"

"Yeah," I answered. I wasn't sure that my legs had built up the strength they needed to do so, but I also wasn't tied to anything.

"Okay, that's good. Do you see any windows? Any light coming through from outside?"

I looked around even though I already knew the answer.

"There aren't any windows. Just a light hanging from the ceiling." I stared at it, hating that the old rusty thing that was barely hanging by a thread was the only light that I had available to me.

"Keep walking; tell me what you see as you walk," he instructed.

I didn't want to tell him that I was too weak to go far, so I tried anyway. I took a few steps and looked around. There was nothing but concrete for what felt like miles.

"There's nothing, Max. It's concrete walls and a concrete floor."

"Do you see any—"

I heard footsteps heading my way and panicked.

"Shhh!" I whispered loudly into the phone.

Whoever it was, came at me quickly, grabbing the phone and pulling it from my hand.

"No! No! Please! Don't!" I begged as they pried my fingers off of it.

The tears started rolling down my face as I heard them say "wrong number" before hanging up. My one chance at freedom was gone.

"You stupid bitch!" a low voice growled before reaching behind and grabbing me by the ponytail. My head jerked back as they tightened their grip on me.

I tried to lift my arms to fight them off when I felt a hand close around my throat, cutting off my air supply. Fingers dug deeper into my flesh, squeezing painfully as I gasped for a breath.

I reached up and clawed at them, desperately trying to make contact with whoever it was. I squirmed and tried to get out of the death grip they had me in. The more I moved, the harder they pressed. In a moment of desperation, I threw my head back, making contact with theirs.

A muttered curse word was all that I heard before they reached up and covered my mouth, making it even harder to breathe.

I tried to suck in a breath but couldn't.

My lungs burned.

My head felt dizzy.

Just one breath, that was all that I needed.

I tried to pull in oxygen through my nose, but the smell of blood was too much for me to handle. It must have been from where I had headbutted them.

The seconds ticked by loudly in my ear as I counted down until I was out of time.

I tried again to take a breath, the fingers wrapped around my mouth so tightly that it felt like my jaw would break.

If I could just get a little bit of oxygen, I might have a chance.

I felt my body start to go numb. My legs shook and trembled as they lost their strength. I could feel my body sinking to the ground as I succumbed to my death.

"Elena, wake up."

I felt fingers on my arm, shaking gently but with urgency.

"Elena, come on, baby, I need you to wake up."

I tried to focus on the voice, the comfort of safety that felt so close yet so far away.

I was so weak, unable to move or open my eyes. I wanted to wake up and see Trevor, to know that I was safe, but I couldn't. I was locked in the dark dungeon of my nightmares, the place that took part of my soul every time I visited it.

A few seconds later—hell, maybe it was minutes or hours, who knew at this point—I felt a cold washcloth on my chest.

"Take a deep breath, Elena. Listen to my voice, you're safe."

I felt the darkness start to lift, the heaviness on my body suddenly gone. I shot up on the bed, panting as I looked around, sucking in as much oxygen as I could.

Trevor was sitting beside me, concern etched across his brow. The washrag sat beside him where it felt when I jolted up.

"You're okay," he said softly and calmly. "Just take a deep breath and focus on my voice."

I tried to do as he instructed as I wildly searched the room, looking for Adam. I knew that he wasn't there, but that never stopped me from searching for him. My breathing was still erratic as I pulled in as many breaths as possible, afraid that I would be deprived of them again.

My body was trembling as I sat in bed, trying to regain control. I hated having these attacks and hated even more that a year later, they hadn't gotten any better. Even though I had stayed at Trevor's apartment more times than I had stayed at my own, it still felt foreign and strange to me right now.

"Look around and tell me five things that you see," Trevor

offered.

I felt silly every time we did this, but it actually helped.

"When you're ready," he added as he climbed up the bed to sit next to me. He gave me plenty of space without touching me as he leaned back against the padded headboard.

I sucked in a deep breath and held it before I slowly pushed it out. My pulse was still racing, and my fingers trembled against my thighs as I sat there, trying to force my mind to focus on the room around me.

"Water bottle, picture frame, television, phone, and blanket." I kept my eyes focused ahead of me and didn't turn to look at him. I knew that he was there if I needed him, but right now, I needed to concentrate on my breathing and getting the oxygen back into my lungs.

"Tell me four things you can touch."

His voice was calming, and it felt like we had done this a thousand times. Maybe we had? I lost track a while ago.

I took another breath, this one more jagged than the last. I dug my fingers into the blanket as I tried to push the anxiety down. It was just a dream, that was all.

My voice trembled as I answered, "The bed, the rug, the curtains, and you."

I heard a low chuckle and felt myself relax a little bit. Not enough to release my death grip on the blanket, but enough to allow me to take a deeper breath in.

"Now, tell me three things that you can hear."

I looked around the room, keeping my head still while my

body worked on getting back to normal. Besides the blood pulsing past my ears, I couldn't hear much.

I watched as the TV on the dresser in front of me turned on, the volume bar at the bottom changing as Trevor turned it up.

My lips twitched as a smile started to pull across my face. If there was ever a reason to love Trevor, it was his constant support with whatever I was going through.

"The TV, the radio, and the rain outside," I answered, letting my eyes wander over to the window that was splattered with raindrops.

"You're doing great," he said, shifting beside me as he crossed his ankle over the other in front of him. "Let's keep going. Two things that you can smell."

My shoulders relaxed some as I took a deep breath, this time feeling the air fill my lungs fully before I slowly let it out. I glanced over at the bag of stuff from the store he had bought earlier and smiled.

"Lotion and body wash."

"That's cheating," he laughed, knowing that I was referring to the items in the bag.

I shrugged, feeling relieved that my body was finally starting to regulate itself.

"Alright, last one," he said soothingly. "One thing you can taste."

I turned to look at him over my shoulder and grinned.

"You."

He chewed on his bottom lip and smiled back at me.

"You already used that one."

I rolled my eyes and slid back on the bed, leaning into his shoulder as I gently nudged him.

"What can I say? You're something I like to touch and taste."

He lifted his arm and pulled me into his side before planting a kiss on the top of my head.

"Right back at you," he replied.

"Thank you," I sighed, thankful for the ease of the breath that floated so effortlessly through me.

"You don't need to thank me."

I sat quietly next to him, focusing on nothing but how I felt beside him. Relaxed. Comfortable. Safe.

"That one didn't last as long as the others," I commented, knowing that he was fully aware of how long my panic attacks could last.

"Have you been having them again lately?" he asked as he gently rubbed his fingers up and down my arm.

I shook my head, partly lying to him. It wasn't panic *attacks* that I was having, but more so staying in a constant state of panic. It was like one huge attack that never ended, and I had no idea what to do about it.

"I know that everyone is just waiting for me to have one and fall apart," I admitted, tucking my chin into his chest to hide my face. "And honestly, I feel like I'm waiting for the same thing."

"It's okay if it happens, Elena. We're all here to help you through it."

I waited a few minutes and thought about what to say before answering.

"I'm afraid that if I fall apart, no one will ever be able to put me back together again. I'm tired of being the broken girl that everyone always has to worry about."

He squeezed me tighter against his body as the tears fell down my face. It felt good to confess this to him, almost as if a weight had been lifted.

"You will never be that girl, Elena. I promise you."

"How do you know," I asked, tilting my head up to look at him. "What if these panic attacks never stop? What if I can't ever move past what happened with Adam? I'm not the same person I was before it happened, and I'm scared of who I might turn into."

He looked down at me with sadness in his eyes.

"I've seen the people that break. You're not one of them." He looked away before saying anything more. "It's late. We should get some sleep."

I nodded and wondered what he was hiding. There was more to what he had said, and I was determined to find out what it was.

Nineteen

Trevor

3 Days Ago

I woke up at five, having slept off and on after waking up around three to help Elena with her panic attack. She was still sleeping soundly in the bed beside me, her breathing even and gentle, which was a relief compared to what it had been earlier.

I moved around the room quietly to keep from waking her up. It was Thursday morning, and I had a pile of work stacked up on my desk, waiting for me to get to it. I sent Roman a quick text message to let him know that I would be in late this morning. While I hated missing work and staying later tonight, it was more important to make sure she was okay this morning.

Elena had been having panic attacks since her kidnapping, but they had started to die off a few months ago. We all had hoped that they were finally going away and that her therapy sessions were helping her to process and work through what had happened. If I could give her anything in the world, it would be to relieve her of the demons that continued to haunt her.

Watching her struggle last night was hard. In the six months that we had been dating, Elena had had several nightmares, but none of them were at the level or intensity of what she had last night. She was gasping in her sleep, pushing away and swatting at me as I tried to wake her up. I could feel the panic radiating off her, and every second that passed before she woke up sent my anxiety further through the roof.

I wasn't even sure if I would be able to pull her out of her attack with our usual methods, but it was all I had at the time. Her panic attack not only affected her, but it also triggered memories that I had worked tirelessly to bury deep beneath the layers of grief.

When she asked how I knew that she wouldn't always be the broken girl that no one could fix, I didn't want to tell her how I could promise her such a thing. I didn't want to tell her that I had known that girl or that I had tried to save that girl but couldn't. Losing Natasha was a pain that I had never been able to dull, and I carried the weight of her death around with me as if I was the one who had pulled the trigger that night.

I shook my head to clear the image from my mind and walked to the kitchen to start a pot of coffee. I wasn't sure what Elena's plans were for the day, but I couldn't imagine that they didn't involve coffee. Once the coffee was started, I headed into the living room to sit down and answer a few emails. I turned on my laptop and waited for it to start up.

As I waited, a new text message from Max came through.

Max: How are things going with Elena?

I scrubbed a hand down my face and reread the message, wondering how to respond. Did I tell him that we had a great night together before she had one of the worst panic attacks I had ever seen? Did I mention that she confessed that she was worried she was heading toward a breakdown and feared that she would never recover from it? It was hard to know how much to tell him and how much to keep to myself at this point.

Me: She's fine. Sleeping.

It didn't take long until I saw the dots bounce across the screen as he replied.

Max: Have you asked her about the other guy?

I blew out a frustrated breath and set my phone down. I knew that I needed to talk to her about it—mainly because everyone was down my throat telling me to talk to her about it. Between Roman and Max, I wasn't sure who was more annoying with their constant requests for updates on it.

I had planned to ask Elena about him, but every time I tried to bring it up, something would distract us, or it just felt like it wasn't the right time because we were fighting. It didn't help that I hadn't seen her much lately and refused to have that conversation through text messages.

Everyone seemed to think that I was fine because I wasn't losing my shit over it. What they didn't know was that I had been livid when I saw her with someone else. So much so that I had to spend the next day patching up the hole in the wall where I had punched my fist through it after I got home. I'd spent time burning off some of my anger at the gym, but even that wasn't enough.

I heard my phone ding again and picked it up to find a text message from Roman.

Roman: I'll get started on the reports, and we can talk

about them when you get here.

I worked my jaw back and forth, remembering the mess I had made and hadn't had a chance to fix. Instead of talking to him about it yesterday, I stormed off and spent the night with Elena. Apparently, my priorities were getting mixed up along with everything else in my life these days.

I sent Roman a text message back before responding to Max.

Me: No, not yet.

Max: You need to talk to her.

Me: I'm aware.

I didn't have time to get into everything through text messages this morning and wanted to change the subject before getting myself worked up and angry again. *If* I decided to talk to her about it this morning, I didn't want to be heated before we even started.

Max: I just want you guys to figure this out and be happy.

You and me both.

An hour later, I was on my third cup of coffee and starting a new pot when Elena walked out of my bedroom. Her hair was a wild mess on the top of her head as she rubbed at her eyes. She was wearing one of my t-shirts with nothing underneath.

"Good morning," I said, trying to keep the thickness out of my voice as I tried to swallow. She stretched, raising her arms above her head as the shirt rode up and barely covered her.

"Morning," she sighed, leaning side to side as she pulled her body in ways that made me want to ravage her.

I cleared my throat and lifted my mug to my lips, allowing the hot liquid to burn my lips as I forced myself to look away.

"Shouldn't you be heading to work?" she asked as she sauntered toward the coffee pot and filled her cup.

"I'm going in late today," I said as I pressed send on my email before exiting it and turning off my computer. I put it on the coffee table and walked over to join her.

"You don't have to babysit me," she muttered before taking a sip of coffee.

I walked behind and snaked my arm around her waist before I leaned in to whisper in her ear.

"No one is babysitting you. I just wanted to make sure you were okay this morning."

She looked up at me over the rim of her mug as she eyed me suspiciously.

"What do you have on your agenda today?" I asked, changing the subject.

"I have work at eleven."

"Are you working late again tonight?" I tried to keep the concern out of my voice, but I hated her working late nights, especially when she had to go home by herself.

She finished taking another drink before setting her mug on the counter.

"I'll be closing, yes."

I heard the sharp tone in her words, but it was the way she narrowed her eyes at me and held her hand on her hip that let me know that she wasn't in the mood to have this argument. Again.

I sighed and leaned back against the counter, folding my arms over my chest.

"I just hate you going home late to an empty apartment."

"I know, you've told me."

"You can stay here with me if you want," I offered, hoping that she would finally reconsider.

"I can't just live here, Trevor," she groaned and shook her head.

"Why not?"

I had been asking Elena to move in with me before she ever signed the lease on her apartment. We didn't fight about much—until recently—but this was the one thing that always seemed to divide us.

"Because I'm not ready to live with you. I love spending time with you here, but I also like having my own space and being independent. You know how big of a deal this is to me."

I pushed off of the counter and walked to her, pulling her into my chest.

She didn't fight me as I held her against me and rubbed my hands up and down her back.

"I'm not pushing you, it was just an offer. I know that you're working later hours for the holidays, and sometimes it's scary going to an empty apartment that late at night."

She laughed against my chest then looked up at me.

"Since when are you scared of anything?"

I swallowed and tried to push away the memories of how terrified I was when she went missing. It was a pain that I had never felt before—not even with Natasha—and never wanted to feel again.

"We all have our weaknesses, Elena."

I watched the same curious look cross her face and pulled away before she could ask me about it.

"We better get ready, or neither of us is going to make it to work today." I reached down and swatted her bare ass, loving the sound as it echoed around us.

She jumped and turned to look at me, a mischievous grin on her face.

"You're going to kill me with all of this sex lately," she giggled, walking over and running her hand along the front of my sweats.

"Last night was a fun night," I agreed, vividly remembering her body trembling against my tongue as her orgasm ripped through her.

"I think we've had more sex this week than in the six months that we've been together."

She laughed and patted me on the chest before walking off to my bedroom. I followed after her, confused by her statement.

"We've had more sex than that," I countered, furrowing my

brow. "Twice in one night isn't a new record for us."

"No," she laughed, "but some of the other stuff you've done recently is definitely new and unexpected."

I watched a blush creep up her neck before it kissed her cheeks. She turned and looked away, seeming embarrassed by something.

Now I was really confused because last night was the first time we had been together since before everything started happening. Maybe she was confusing her sexcapades with the other guy instead of me? The thought sent fire through my veins as I balled my hands into fists at my side.

"What are you talking about?" I bit out with more anger than I had intended.

She pulled her head back and gave me a strange look.

"You know what I'm talking about, Trevor." She sat down on the edge of the bed and crossed her arms. "I know that we've been avoiding talking about it, but I think it's time that we just clear the air about it and move forward."

I swallowed hard, my Adam's apple pushing tightly in my throat. So that was how we were going to approach this thing with the other guy—like it wasn't a big deal?

"Well, I've been waiting to talk to you about it but haven't found the right time." I worked my jaw back and forth, waiting for her to respond.

"It's funny because I've been waiting to talk to you about it, but every time I do, you seem to change the topic or find some way to distract me, so we can't."

My brow wrinkled in confusion.

"Are you messing with me right now?" I asked.

"Messing with you? Why would I be messing with you? If anyone has been messing with anyone, it's been *you* messing with *me*."

I leaned against the wall and ran a hand down my face.

"What in the world are you talking about, Elena? We've hardly seen each other in—I don't even know how long now. Since the charger incident at your apartment? How could I possibly be messing with you?"

She tilted her head back and laughed. Not just a sarcastic laugh, but a manic laugh that started to worry me that she really was about to lose it.

"I don't know why I expected anything different," she muttered, shaking her head. "Fits in with everything else you've been doing lately."

"That *I've* been doing? You're the one who's been seeing someone else, Elena! And you didn't even bother to talk to me about it. Maybe all of the sex you think we've been having was really you with this other guy!" My voice boomed through the room, causing her to flinch in response.

"What the hell are you talking about? I haven't been seeing anyone but you."

I arched a brow and stared at her, unable to believe that she was sitting right in front of me, lying to me.

"I saw you, Elena," I said firmly through gritted teeth.

"When?"

"Last week. You seemed mad at me after the charger

incident at your house and wouldn't talk to me through text. I decided to bring you flowers to apologize for whatever I had done wrong, and as I was getting in the elevator, I saw you leaving with another guy."

Her face went blank as she stared at me.

"I haven't been with another guy, Trevor. And you know that."

I shook my head, trying to force some of the frustration out.

"Are you calling me a liar?" I asked. "Because I know what I saw, Elena."

"I don't know what you are," she said sternly as she stood up and took a few steps away from me. "But I know that this isn't the only weird thing that you've been doing lately, and I'm over these games."

"What else have I done?" I questioned, throwing my hands up in the air.

"What haven't you done?" she scoffed. "It's like you're determined to make me look crazy. Like you're purposely doing things to make me think that I'm losing my mind. You're the one forcing me into these breakdowns that I keep having, and I don't know why. What's in it for you, Trevor? Do you need to be the hero again and save the day? Does your ego need that much boosting that you would risk my sanity to get it?"

I pushed off of the wall and took a step toward her before I saw the panic flash through her eyes. I stopped and pointed at her.

"You know that I would *never* do anything like that. Why in the world would you ever say that?"

"Because you're driving me crazy, Trevor. *Literally crazy*! You text me when we're standing right next to each other. You act like you have no idea what I'm talking about, even when we just talked about it the other day. And then the whole choking incident—that was too far, Trevor, and you knew it."

The color drained from my face as I watched her start to lose it in front of me. Was this the breakdown that Max was worried she would have?

"What choking incident?" I asked, worried about what she was going to say. Was she making this shit up, or did she really believe it had happened?

She put her hand on her hip and stared at me with one brow arched.

"You know what I'm talking about."

"I can guarantee you that I don't."

She rolled her eyes and looked around the room as if she was searching for the answer. Finally, she focused on me again and looked me in the eye with a look of satisfaction on her face.

"Alright, then I'll show you. I have it on video."

Things were unraveling faster than I could try to hold them together.

"You have what on video?"

"Us having sex on Friday night and you choking me until right before I came."

I felt a chill run down my spine as my head was

overwhelmed with questions that I needed to ask but didn't know where to start.

"Let's go," I said, stepping aside so she could leave the room.

"Where?" she asked, her anger still radiating through the room.

"To see that video."

<u>Twenty</u>
Elena
3 Days Ago

The trip to my apartment was quick but felt like forever, given how tense things were between us. Neither of us bothered to talk, our anger too heavy to deal with at the moment. I tapped my fingers impatiently on the rail in the elevator, waiting for it to hurry up and get to my floor. Once the doors opened, I pushed off and walked out, not bothering to check where Trevor was behind me. Even though I could see his nostrils flare, I could still sense his overprotectiveness radiating off of him.

Once the door was open, I stepped inside and held it, so it didn't slam in his face. I looked around quickly, making sure nothing was out of place. No matter how hard I tried, I still couldn't shake the feeling that someone was constantly coming and going when I wasn't looking.

I heard the door shut behind me and glanced over my shoulder at Trevor. His eyes scanned the room, likely looking for where I had hidden the camera. It gave me a slight sense of satisfaction that he hadn't easily found it, which meant that whoever had been coming and going hadn't found it either. It also meant that he hadn't seen it the other night when we had sex—the night he was acting like never happened.

I was about to walk over to the bookshelf next to the TV when something on the counter caught my eye. I walked over and found an envelope sitting on top of the mail that I hadn't brought up myself. There wasn't anything written on it, just a plain-white, blank envelope.

"So, where is the camera?" Trevor asked, pulling me away from the mysterious object that felt more ominous the longer I stared at it.

I snapped my attention over to him and raised a brow. His impatience was making me feel more irritable than I was already feeling. I walked over to the bookshelf and pulled the textbook out that was hiding the camera. I had taken the time to cut the smallest hole in the bottom of the spine to make sure no one easily spotted it.

When I picked up the book, my heart dropped to the floor. I ran my fingers along the spine that was perfectly intact. I looked at the bookshelf again, double-checking to make sure I hadn't picked up the wrong book. I leaned in and slowly scanned each book, desperate to find the one with the camera.

"Is everything okay?" he asked as he walked over and stood beside me, looking at the book in my hand.

"No," I muttered. "Everything is not okay."

I felt like the world was spinning out of control around me. How had this happened? Had he spotted the camera and snuck into my apartment to get rid of it just to make me look crazy? Aside from Max, Trevor was the only other person who had a key to my apartment, which was given to both of them shortly after the phone charger incident. Before that, no one had access to my place, and I felt a lot safer back then.

"What did you do with it?" I asked, pushing the book back on the bookshelf and placing my hands on my hips.

"Excuse me?" He pulled his head back in shock.

"The camera, Trevor. What did you do with it?"

He stepped back and worked his jaw back and forth. His blue eyes darkened as he looked around helplessly.

"I have no idea what you're talking about, Elena."

My body was heating up with anger as I took a step toward him. I pushed a finger into his chest as I narrowed my eyes and stared at him.

"Stop it with these games. I don't know what you think this is—but I'm not interested in it. Just tell me where the camera is or leave."

Trevor's hand reached up and gently wrapped around my wrist as I continued to poke him. His eyes softened as he looked past me to the coffee table.

"That camera?" he asked, nodding to the box.

I pulled my hand away and spun around. There was no fucking way that this was happening. How did the camera get back in the box, and who the hell had put it on the coffee table? I slowly walked over and picked it up, examining the seal that was still intact on the outside of the box.

"You've got to be kidding me," I muttered as I continued to move the box around, looking for any spots where it might have been opened. The problem was that I clearly remembered taking it out of the package and then throwing everything in the trash once I had it set up. And how on earth did the book get fixed?

"Maybe you thought you had done it but hadn't gotten around to it yet?" Trevor offered, the anger in his voice now replaced with sympathy.

"No!" I shouted, sitting the box back down on the coffee table and turning to look at him. "Trevor, I'm not crazy. I had that camera set up. I watched the video after we had sex—I saw the whole thing."

His brow arched, and I couldn't tell if the smirk that threatened to cross his face was because he thought I was going out of my mind or because he was judging me for making a sex tape and then watching it.

"I didn't watch it because I was being a pervert," I sighed, pushing past the thought. "I watched it because I had seen a notification that there was movement, and I wanted to see what it had picked up."

My mind was going a mile a minute as everything started to fall into place. If the camera was up and had caught Trevor and me having sex, why hadn't I got the notification when someone was in my apartment? Come to think of it– I hadn't gotten any notifications since the sex incident.

I pulled out my phone and unlocked the screen before flipping through to find the app for the camera. I chewed my lip anxiously as I flipped between the two main screens, knowing that I had put it on the first page, right next to my social media icons. I went to my settings and scrolled through the list of apps, my stomach knotting when it wasn't there anymore.

TEN SECONDS TOO LATE

I sat on the edge of the couch and went to the app store, typing in the name of the program. It pulled up the app, and a few minutes later, it was downloading again. Once it was complete, I entered my log-in information and pressed enter. I glanced up at Trevor, knowing that if I couldn't prove that I had the camera set up when we had sex, then he would think he won whatever this was between us.

I looked down at my phone, frowning when it popped up with an error message. I entered my information again and waited for another error message. I tried to reset my password and let out a grunt of frustration when the new message confirmed there was no account on file with that email address.

I sat my phone down on the couch next to me and leaned back, shaking my head in irritation.

"It's okay, we'll figure this out," Trevor said gently as he sat down on the other end of the couch.

I could feel my anxiety building again and knew that I needed to get a handle on this before I felt like it was out of my control.

"I think that you should go," I said sternly with my arms folded across my chest. I didn't bother to look at him, knowing that if I did, I might get lost in the eyes that used to make me feel comfortable and safe.

I watched as his shoulders rose and fell in defeat.

"Elena," he begged. "Please, let's talk about this."

I got up and walked to the door, holding it open for him.

"There's nothing to talk about. I need space, and I need you to leave. I'm not the girl who needs saving anymore, Trevor, so you're going to have to find her somewhere else."

A few seconds passed before he pushed his hands into his thighs and stood up. He shook his head as he walked past me and slipped out the door without saying another word. Once he was gone, I locked and slid down it.

Something was going on, and it was up to me to figure out what it was.

Twenty-One
Trevor
3 Days Ago

"Again, I'm sorry for missing that," I apologized to Roman as we looked over the spreadsheets together.

I stood up and clapped him on the shoulder before I headed back over to my desk. It was a little after three in the afternoon, but it felt like it had been days with how long this day had dragged on after I left Elena's apartment.

I wanted to text her and see how she was doing, but I knew she would reach out to me when she was ready. Unfortunately, I didn't know when that would be. It could be an hour from now. A few weeks. Months. Hell, it could be a year with Elena depending on how mad she was.

Deciding to get caught up on work, I made a fresh pot of coffee and planted my ass in my chair, ignoring anything and everything so I could focus. By six, Roman was packing up to leave for the night when Max strolled in.

"Hey, wanna go grab a beer?" he asked as he leaned against the doorway.

"Can't," I mumbled as I continued to stare at the spreadsheet on my computer. "Another time."

"What's with him?" Max asked Roman as if I wasn't still in the room.

"Don't know. He's been that way all day," Roman answered.

"Did something happen with Elena?" Max asked.

I tried to ignore the question and pretended to be working when I felt their heavy gazes burning holes into my head. I blew out a loud, annoyed breath and pushed the keyboard away from me as I leaned back against my chair.

"She wants space, so I'm giving it to her." I folded my hands across my stomach as I raised my brow at them.

Roman set his stuff down on his desk, no longer in a hurry to go anywhere.

"What does that mean?" Max asked, walking closer to my desk. "What happened?"

"Honestly?" I questioned, not sure that he wanted to hear this any more than I wanted to say it. He nodded, and I let my shoulders fall with the breath that I let out. "I think she's having that mental breakdown that we've all been worried about."

"Is she okay?" Roman asked with genuine concern in his voice.

"I don't know," I admitted. "Things were fine yesterday, then she had a panic attack in the middle of the night."

"Nightmare?" Max inquired.

I pursed my lips and then rubbed them together.

"Yeah, worse than any of the other ones I've seen her have before. I couldn't get her to wake up, and when she finally did, she was gasping for air."

"Was it about Adam?"

I nodded and lowered my eyes.

"Panic attacks are hard," Roman said softly. "Try to give her some time to work through it. It may seem like it's easy to move past it once it's over but trust me when I say that the aftereffects of one can stay with you longer than you'd think."

"That's the thing– it's not just the panic attack. Everything just spiraled out of control after that."

"Like what?" Max asked, sitting in the empty chair in the corner of the room.

"She started accusing me of random things—things that didn't make any sense. She claimed that we had slept together recently, and I thought maybe she was mistaking it for the other guy—so I asked her about him. She got really angry and defensive, claiming that I had tried to choke her during an orgasm," I swallowed hard and looked away from Max as I said it, "and that she had video to prove it."

"She recorded you guys having sex?" Roman asked, his brows shooting up on his forehead.

"No," I shook my head. "At least I don't think she meant to on purpose."

I took a deep breath and backtracked what I was trying to say.

"She claimed that she had the cameras already up, and they caught us having sex. She was going to prove to me that this had happened, but when we got to her apartment so she could show me, the camera wasn't there."

"Like someone took it?" Max questioned.

I leaned forward in my chair and rested my elbows on my desk, rolling my head around my neck a few times to relieve some of the tension that was quickly building.

"No one took it because she never installed it. The camera was still sealed in the box, sitting on her coffee table."

"Did she remember leaving it there once she saw it?" There was a hope in Max's voice that I felt bad for ruining when I said no.

"She got really angry with me and told me to leave. I don't remember her exact words, but she keeps telling me that she's not some girl that needs to be saved. The scary thing is that she's convinced that I'm doing these things to her to make her look crazy so I can turn around and save her. Some sort of ego boost or something, according to her."

"Are you?" Max asked, his jaw tight as he held his hands together in front of him.

I pushed a hand through my hair then glared at him.

"Are you seriously fucking asking me that right now?" I bit out.

"It's a fair question," he replied sternly. "Something is happening, and a lot of it seems to fall back on you."

"What's happening is your sister's life is falling apart right in front of us, and instead of trying to help her, you're standing there pointing fingers as if I would ever do a damn thing to hurt her. The fact that you don't know me better than that says a lot about our friendship."

"I'm her big brother and a detective—it's my job to look at every possibility—"

"Then get the hell out of my office and go do your job."

I met his glare as the tension thickened in the room between us. Max muttered something under his breath before he stood up and walked out.

Roman gave me a nod before picking up his stuff and following behind him, leaving me alone to my misery and silence.

TEN SECONDS TOO LATE

Twenty-Two
Elena
2 Days Ago

I sat nervously outside Natalie's office, waiting for her to finish with her client. I had gotten here early, determined to be focused when I saw her instead of the chaos that I felt bubbling around inside of me.

It was a week until Christmas, and I still hadn't finished any of my shopping. Who could when their whole world felt like it had been turned upside down?

Between the fight with Trevor yesterday and the moldy bologna that was waiting for me in the fridge when I got home from work, I couldn't concentrate on anything other than figuring out what was going on. I had accused Trevor of doing stuff to mess with me so he could look like the hero and save the day, but now I wasn't so sure that I was that far off from the truth.

Out of everything in my fridge that could have been placed in the middle of the empty shelf, waiting for me to find it, was moldy bologna sitting on a plate. Very few people knew that Adam had forced me to eat it when he was punishing me while I was being held against my will. The only people I had shared that information with were Trevor, Max, and Hannah.

Call me crazy—oh wait, he already did—but out of the three of them, he was starting to look more like the culprit after all.

Ten minutes later, I sat against the wall and watched as a woman walked out of Natalie's office, blotting her eyes with a tissue as she headed toward the door. I forced myself to relax as Abby sat at her desk; her eyes narrowed at the computer screen as she reached her hand out to answer the phone that was ringing beside her.

"Yes," she said quietly, glancing up to look at me before looking away. "Okay. Yes. Will do."

I felt my heart sink to my stomach when she turned and looked at me, folding her hands in front of her on her desk.

"I'm sorry, Elena, Natalie will have to reschedule. She's had something come up."

I swallowed hard, pushing my emotions to the back of my throat as my blood pressure started to rise.

"Did she say what it was?" I asked, my voice hoarse and scratchy.

"Unfortunately, that's not information that I can discuss. However, if you'd like, I can see what she has available next week?"

"Next week," I repeated numbly. There was no way that I could go that long without talking to her.

She nodded and tried to smile sympathetically.

"Don't bother," I mumbled under my breath before grabbing my purse from the chair beside me and getting up.

"Elena..." she called out as I stormed out of the office,

letting the door slam behind me.

My heart was racing as I rushed down the stairs, not bothering to wait for the elevator. It felt like the walls were closing in around me, the air thick as I tried to take in a breath.

Just a few more steps, that's all you have to go before you're outside and can take a deep breath.

I pushed my legs to move faster, nearly tripping on the last few steps, forcing me out into the lobby with a force that drew the attention of the few people who were in there.

I tucked my chin to my chest and hurried out, avoiding the curious glances of the onlookers around me. Once outside, I took a step out of the way and leaned against the wall, sucking in as much air as I could while my legs trembled beneath me.

My whole body was on high alert, ready to run again if needed. It wasn't unusual for me to go into this mode when my anxiety spiraled out of control, but for once, the tingle that traveled up my spine told me that I had a reason to run.

I looked around, surveilling the area as I searched for any possible threats. It was a silly thing to do given that this was New York City, and even the rapists and murderers blended in easily with the tourists and business people rushing to wherever they needed to go.

I pushed off the wall and turned to head to the subway when I hit a solid wall of muscle. Strong arms wrapped around me, holding me steady as I slowly looked up, wondering who I had just barreled into.

Roman looked down at me with concern etched on his face.

His brows pulled down, making his brown eyes look darker in the shade of the skyscraper beside us. I tried to steady my breathing but couldn't.

"Are you okay?" he asked, his hands still holding me upright as my legs threatened to give out on me at that moment.

"Yeah, I'm fine," I replied, knowing that I was lying through my teeth. Whether he knew it or not, that was another question. I had met Roman a handful of times with Trevor, but this was the first time we had ever talked by ourselves.

He didn't say anything, just continued to stare at me as his eyes searched for whatever he was looking for.

"I um, better get going." I tucked a strand of hair behind my ear and stepped back. I avoided eye contact for fear of what he must be thinking about me right now.

Had Trevor been talking to him about me? Did he know about all of the crazy things that had been happening? Even worse—did he think that I was crazy? I definitely wasn't making a good impression at the moment as I jittered around more anxious than a drug addict trying to pass a drug test in front of a cop.

When he continued to stare in silence, I pulled my lips into a thin line, trying to force a smile to appear before I stepped to the side to walk away.

I got half of a step past him when I felt him grab my arm and stop me.

"Are you sure you're fine?" he asked, his voice tenser than before.

"Yeah," I nodded as enthusiastically as I could. "Just late for work."

It was as if I couldn't stop lying. They were flying out of my mouth quicker than I could stop them. I had the day off and planned to go home and catch up on sleep if my mind would let me.

I gently pulled out of his grip and gave him a tight smile before shoving my hands in my pockets and walking away. Once I was a few blocks past him, I let out the rugged breath that I had been holding and made my way to the subway. While I had been expecting something creepy to happen on my way home, I was pleasantly surprised by the noneventful trip back.

Maybe I was going to be able to get that sleep after all.

I got off the elevator and walked down the hall that led to my apartment, wondering who the guy in the leather jacket on the other side was. He didn't look familiar, but he had his head down, looking at his phone as I approached.

Since he didn't seem at all aware that I was there, I slid past him, unlocked the door, and slipped inside before closing it quickly behind me. I flipped the locks into place and tossed my purse on the counter as I kicked my shoes off and toed them over to the corner.

I headed to the bathroom, allowing my eyes to close for a brief moment as a yawn forced its way through my overly exhausted body. When I opened them, I gasped and clutched my hand to my chest as I jumped back a step.

"Max!" I yelled, still holding my chest as if I was afraid my heart would leap right out of my body. "What the hell are you doing here?!"

His fingers moved swiftly across his phone before he locked it and tucked it into the pocket of his jeans. He leaned casually against the door as if he hadn't just scared the soul out of my body. I wasn't sure if this was what people meant by an out-of-body experience, but it sure as hell felt like one to me.

I raised an eyebrow while I waited for him to answer me.

"I came to check on you."

His voice was even– nothing in his tone to give me any more information than that.

"You could have called," I replied sternly.

"I did," he said, nodding to my phone sticking out of the jacket of my hoodie. "You didn't answer."

I pulled my phone out and found two missed calls from him.

"So that automatically means that you just show up and let yourself into my apartment?"

"I don't play around when it comes to your safety."

I rolled my eyes and snorted.

"How long are you going to hold that against me?" he asked, folding his arms tighter across his chest.

"What?"

"Not saving you in time with Adam."

My heart leaped into my throat, proving again that it had no idea where in my body it was really supposed to be.

This wasn't something that we had talked about before. In fact, aside from Natalie, I hadn't talked to anyone about the feelings that I harbored against Max when it came to my kidnapping. It wasn't like it was his fault, yet I had this anger that lingered around every time I thought about how I had him on the phone, and yet he still couldn't find me. He was always my superhero when I was growing up, but I learned the hard way that his powers only worked with make-belief play.

"I don't know what you're talking about," I said as another lie spewed out of my mouth.

I turned around and walked over to the couch as he followed me. Pretending that I wasn't bothered by the conversation, I reached for the remote and turned on the TV.

"Stop with the bullshit, Elena," he snapped, plopping down in the chair across from me. "We can keep pretending that you don't hate me for what happened, or we can talk about it and work through it."

"There's nothing to talk about," I replied with my eyes still laser-focused on the TV.

"Yes, there is," he pushed.

I could feel the tension building between us from the words we refused to speak.

"You can easily see that I'm safe," I said, changing the subject while still avoiding eye contact.

"You don't have to stay. I'm sure Hannah needs you at home."

"You're as stubborn as Ma," he grumbled as he leaned back and worked his jaw.

My eyes darted over to his, the anger radiating off of me.

"What did you just say?"

He leaned forward and rested his arms on his knees.

"I said that you're as stubborn as Ma," he repeated.

"Wow," I blew out, shaking my head in disbelief. "I can't believe that you went there."

"Well, someone had to tell you the truth."

I narrowed my eyes and gave him the silent treatment.

After a few minutes, he blew out an irritated breath and stood up.

"Alright, fine. If you don't want to talk, I won't make you. But someday, you're going to have to face the demons that haunt you, Elena. And that means talking to me about the anger and resentment you have for me over Adam."

I bit the inside of my cheek to try to force the tears from stinging my eyes.

"I would have come for you right then and there, Leni. If I would have known where you were, I would have come for you. There wasn't a damn thing in the world that could have kept me from getting there. We did *everything* that we could to find you. Every damn thing."

His shoulders rose and fell as he turned to walk away. He stopped in his tracks and looked down at the coffee table, spotting the picture sitting on top of it.

Something about the way his fingers trembled as he reached down to pick it up sent a chill through me. He held it up to his face and covered his mouth with his other hand. Max had always been the strong, rugged brother who didn't show his emotions often, so his reaction to the photo caught me completely off guard.

"Where did you get this?" he asked as he kept staring at it.

I paused for a moment, not sure of what to say. *It was left for me in my apartment by whoever keeps sneaking in to fuck with me?*

When I still hadn't answered a few minutes later, he turned around to face me and looked directly at me when he asked, "Where did you get this picture, Elena?"

There was a warning in his tone.

"It was left in my apartment."

"By who?"

"I don't know?" I shrugged, telling the truth for once today.

He went back to staring at the picture, ignoring everything around him. His phone started ringing, but he didn't make any effort to pull it out of his pocket and answer it.

"Who is she?" I asked, leaning forward on the couch as I waited nervously for the answer.

"Natasha." Her name rolled off of his lips in a whisper that I could barely hear.

I waited for him to go on, having never heard of her before now. It was evident that she was important to him, or he wouldn't have had that reaction to her photo.

His phone started ringing again, this time pulling him out of his trance enough for him to check it but not answer it.

"Who is Natasha?"

He sat down, sitting the photo on his knee as if he was afraid to lose it.

"She was Trevor's sister."

"Was?" I questioned, feeling a chill wrap around me.

"She died ten years ago."

My stomach sank with sadness as I leaned back against the couch.

"I didn't know that he had a sibling," I admitted, instantly feeling bad that I hadn't known this about him. We had known each other for years and had been dating for six months—you would think that I would know if he had any siblings—dead or alive.

"He had two," he said sadly. "Triplets. One girl and two boys."

My head was spinning as I tried to process this information. Why had he never mentioned anything about his family before? I knew that his dad left when he was a kid and that his mom was always a single mother, never bothering to remarry, but you would think that he would talk about his siblings, especially being a triplet.

"Where's his brother?"

I knew better than to ask the questions that I didn't really want the answers to, but deep inside, I needed to know. The man that I thought I knew better than anyone was quickly turning into someone that I didn't know at all.

Max's face fell even more when he closed his eyes and shook his head.

"Hunter died a few years ago."

"What?" I whispered, covering my mouth in shock.

How could there be so much death and sadness in one family?

"Car accident."

"What happened to his sister?" I asked quietly, ashamed that my curiosity was getting the best of me.

"She killed herself." He pulled in a heavy breath and slowly let it out. "She used to have terrible panic attacks that Trevor would try to help her with. In the end, it was just too much for her, and she couldn't take it anymore. She was convinced that someone was stalking her and trying to make her look crazy."

He stopped talking and looked up at me as if he knew that his words had triggered my own feelings of being crazy lately. But if anything, everything suddenly made sense. I closed my eyes and pinched the bridge of my nose.

"That's what he was referring to," I said as the puzzle all finally clicked into place.

"What who was referring to?" Max asked, confused.

"Trevor," I sighed. "I had a panic attack while I was at his apartment the other night. I told him that I was afraid of becoming someone I didn't know—someone who couldn't be saved. He told me that he's seen people that break and that I wasn't one of them."

"Her death was hard for everyone, but Trevor took it the hardest. He had it ingrained in his mind that he had to be the one to save her. When he couldn't, he took that to heart and never forgave himself for it."

My heart broke for Trevor as I felt the weight of the grief that he continued to carry around with him.

Max's phone rang again, interrupting our conversation. He pulled it out and sighed before looking up at me.

"It's Hannah; she's still sick. I need to go by and check on her."

"Okay," I nodded as I got up and walked with him to the door.

He shoved his phone back into his pocket and grabbed his coat that had been hanging on the coat rack.

"Did Trevor ever figure out what was happening to her?" I blurted out before I could think it through.

Max furrowed his brow as he shrugged into his coat.

"What do you mean?"

"You said that she thought someone was stalking her and trying to make her look crazy. Did Trevor ever figure out who was doing it?"

His face fell as he looked down at the floor before raising his eyes to meet mine.

"She was convinced that it was him."

Twenty-Three
Trevor
2 Days Ago

"Cheers to Thirsty Thursday!" The blond girl with fake boobs pushed up to her chin yelled as she slammed her shot glass into the girl beside her, laughing hysterically as the alcohol sloshed all over them.

I rolled my eyes and lifted my beer to my lips, trying to tune them and their obnoxious behavior out. It had already been a long day, and I was ready to call it quits. Had Max not sent me a text, asking me to meet up, I would have already been home and probably in bed. I glanced down at my watch, grimacing at the thought given that it was barely after six-thirty.

Jon shook his head at the girls as he wiped down a glass with a towel before sitting it on the shelf behind the bar. A few minutes later, the front door opened and the light filtered in from outside, nearly blinding me in the dimly lit room. Max made his way over and gave Jon a quick nod before taking off his jacket and sitting down on the barstool across the table from me.

I took another sip, not bothering to say anything. It wasn't like we weren't going to talk about what had happened yesterday. I just wasn't ready to deal with it yet. I had a massive headache that had controlled most of my day, not to mention the stress of trying to get things ready for Christmas since it was right around the corner. Even though I wasn't huge on doing anything big for the holiday, I knew that it was important to my mom, and that was reason enough to make it a big deal for me.

Jon came over and dropped off Max's beer before walking over and tending to the drunk girls in the corner.

"Have they been here long?" Max asked with a nod in their direction as he lifted the bottle to his lips and took a drink.

"Long enough to be celebrating *Thirsty Thursday*," I muttered.

I could see the wheels turning in his head as he tried to shift from cop mode to friend mode.

"They're probably just burning off some steam from finals. You know that Jon wouldn't serve minors, and he's seen so many fake IDs that no one even bothers trying to use them here anymore," I commented, saving Max from the hassle of trying to solve a problem that we didn't need right now.

He shrugged as if he didn't care and took another drink before turning his attention back to me.

"How's Hannah?" I asked casually.

I hated the tension that lingered between us, covering us in a blanket of awkwardness that wasn't natural. If we had beef with each other, we'd always just deal with it and move on. But, now that it involved Elena, it felt like neither of us knew how to navigate the new territory.

"She's on the mend, finally keeping food down," he replied as he set his bottle down on the table in front of me. "Is that who you really wanted to ask about?" He gave me a pointed look as he read my mind.

I let my head hang, feeling the ache in my neck and shoulders from the stress that wouldn't leave no matter how hard I tried.

"How is she?" I finally asked, looking up at him.

He waited before answering, making me squirm with anticipation. There hadn't been a moment since I walked out of her apartment that I hadn't thought about her. The fact that she had asked for space from me had shattered whatever was left of my broken heart. It would be stupid to say that it had ever been whole when I had given it to her, to begin with.

"She's fine," he answered, his eyes wandering back over to the group of girls that were pouting and sticking their bottom lip out at Jon as he cut them off.

"That's all you're going to give me?" I asked with a sarcastic laugh tied in.

"If you want to know more, you should ask her yourself."

"She told me to give her space. She's made it real clear that she wants nothing to do with me right now."

"Maybe it's because you left a picture of a girl in her apartment and didn't bother to tell her who it was?"

I pulled my head back and furrowed my brow.

"What the hell are you talking about?"

He narrowed his eyes at me as his jaw tightened.

"You know what the hell I'm talking about. That was a dick move, Trevor."

"Are you kidding me right now?"

I caught Jon's eye as he walked past and nodded to my beer, asking for another. It was obvious that I was going to need more to get through whatever this was with Max.

He tilted his head to the side as he studied me.

"She was right about not needing to be saved– you know that, right?" he asked with a stern tone.

"You're not making any sense right now," I muttered, scrubbing a hand over the stubble that had popped up over my jaw the past few days.

"She's not Natasha, Trevor. So you can stop all of the bullshit. I know that it's coming up on the tenth anniversary since she died, but there's no reason to bring Elena into this. If you need to see a therapist and work through your unresolved grief, so be it. But leave my sister the fuck out of it. It's not fair to her, especially after everything she's already been through, and you of all people should know that."

He stood up and pulled out his wallet before tossing a twenty-dollar bill on the table.

"Seriously—what the fuck are you talking about?" I asked as my head spun.

"You left a picture of Natasha in her apartment. You've been obsessed about Elena needing help and trying to save her. I should have seen it before," he sighed as he ran a hand through his hair. "But now that I know what's going on, I'm here to put a stop to it. Leave my sister out of your bullshit. I won't tell you again."

He tapped his knuckles on the table, then turned around and left. Jon gave me a puzzled look as he set my beer down in front of me.

"Is he coming back?" he asked.

I shook my head and picked up my beer, not bothering to explain because that would mean that I had some sort of idea of what the fuck had just happened.

Twenty-Four
Elena
2 Days Ago

I woke up feeling more rested than I had in days, though my dreams were enough to make me not want to sleep again. Shortly after Max left, I laid down and willed myself to sleep. Finally, after however many hours, I fell asleep. I was in such a deep sleep that I hadn't heard my phone ring seven times or the notifications from the numerous voicemails that my mother had left me, checking on me and trying to confirm what my plans were for Christmas Eve.

It was the first year that I didn't live at home during the holidays, and she was struggling with trying to keep some of the traditions alive. It wasn't like she hadn't gone through this with my other sisters as they started leaving the house, but it felt like it was a lot different since I was the baby. A few of my sisters still lived there, so there was no reason that she couldn't keep the tradition alive with them, but that was a fight to have with her another day.

I rolled out of bed and set my phone down on the nightstand. Trevor hadn't called or texted me, which left me feeling a little disappointed, even though I had been the one to tell him that I wanted space. Of course, that didn't mean that I hadn't hoped that he would ignore me and still try to get a hold of me. I mean, come on, is fighting for the person that you love too much to ask for?

The clock on the wall confirmed that it was a little after eight and that I had slept the majority of the day away. It was great that I had caught up on the rest that I needed, but it also sucked because that meant that I would be up late tonight and had to get up early for work tomorrow.

I decided to take a shower before rummaging through the kitchen to find something to eat. My mind was still fuzzy as I tried to process everything Max had told me when he was here earlier. I walked absentmindedly to my dresser and grabbed clean underwear before pulling a hoodie and some yoga pants out of my closet.

The hot water was soothing, helping me relax as I tried to unwind from the past few weeks. I was confident that I would still be anxious until I talked to Natalie, but for some reason, talking to Max earlier had helped to calm me down. Maybe it was because I felt like I finally had some of the answers that I had been looking for with Trevor. Even as confusing as everything was, it felt like it was all starting to make sense.

I now understood why he was so good at helping me through my panic attacks but would never have guessed that it was because he used to do it for his sister. Knowing the guilt that he carried over her suicide made me realize that he was feeling desperate as he watched me struggle with my own anxiety. He must have been worried that I was going down the same path that she had, and the fear of history repeating itself would make anyone do something crazy. Even if that meant stalking your current girlfriend and making her look insane, just so you could swoop in and feel like you saved her.

I stayed under the hot water for a few more minutes before I reluctantly turned it off and grabbed the towel off of the hook beside the shower. I quickly wrapped it around me and pulled my hair into another one while I dried off. The heat seemed to be fluctuating in the apartment again, but it was likely due to the storm that was coming in. Unfortunately, it seemed like we weren't going to get any breaks with the weather before Christmas with bitter cold storms, one on top of another.

I pulled the curtain back and stepped out of the shower before looking around for the clothes I had brought in. The towel started slipping down my body, so I tucked the corner in tighter and bent down, spotting them on the floor under the toilet. They must have fallen off when I grabbed the towel.

I got dressed and hung the towel up on the hook by the door, and headed to the kitchen to find something to eat. It was a silly thing to do, given that I already knew that I didn't have anything decent to eat. I could always go over to my mom's house and raid her fridge, but it was getting late, and I didn't want to scare her if I showed up randomly, looking for food.

Closing the fridge, I gave up and grabbed my keys and phone so I could go grab something close by. As I walked into the hallway and locked the door, I spotted the same guy from this morning sitting outside the door across the hall from me. It seemed strange that he was still there, but it didn't bother me enough to ask him about it. It wasn't like he was hanging out around my door or trying to get into my apartment.

Ignoring the nagging feeling that I should be more worried about who was hanging around my apartment, I got in the elevator and pressed the button to go down to the lobby. The doors opened a few minutes later, and I headed down the street to the deli on the corner.

It was freezing outside, and I instantly regretted not bundling up in something warmer before I left. My hoodie was warm but not thick enough to shield me from the wind as it whipped past me. I pushed my way inside the store and let the door slam behind me.

The deli was quiet, with just a few people inside. I grabbed a sandwich from the refrigerated section then browsed the chip aisle for something to go with it. As I walked up to the front, I browsed the wine selection, wishing that I wasn't fighting with Trevor right now so he could buy me another bottle. It's not like it was a secret with Max, but he also wasn't likely to buy his underage sister alcohol. Trevor, on the other hand, didn't mind buying a bottle or two here and there that we would share when he came over.

I waited in line behind a mom and her two kids as they rang up their groceries and paid. It reminded me a lot of my childhood, going to run errands with my mom while my dad was busy working two jobs so she could stay home to take care of us.

Once it was my turn, I headed to the counter and laid my items down. The cashier mumbled something along the lines of hello as she started ringing me up. I glanced around and grabbed a few candy bars before sliding them over with my stuff at the last minute. She waited for me to swipe my card, then tucked my receipt in the paper bag before rolling it closed and handing it to me. I offered a smile before walking away, but it was missed as she focused on the next customer behind me.

The walk back to my apartment was painful as I fought against the weather. I was a few feet away from the door to the lobby when I saw a man in a dark hoodie walk out. Before they could turn around, I caught a glimpse of their face. My heart skipped a beat as I picked up my pace.

"Trevor?" I called out loud enough to notice him stop for a split second before pulling the hood over his head and walking off in the other direction.

I ran after him, pissed that he was acting as if he hadn't heard me call out his name. I dodged a few people who muttered curse words at me along the way, but by the time I got to where he had been, he was gone.

I got in the elevator and headed up to my apartment. When I got there, the man in the leather jacket was no longer there, and my apartment door was wide open.

TEN SECONDS TOO LATE

Twenty-Five
Trevor
1 Day Ago

"So, what brings you in to see me today?" Natalie asked as she subtly tilted her head to the side and leaned back in her leather office chair.

I looked around the room, suddenly feeling like it was smaller than the last time when I was here with Elena. I hadn't planned on calling and begging for an appointment this morning, but I was thankful when they had a last-minute cancellation a few minutes before, and Natalie agreed to squeeze me in.

"I'm sorry, I don't really know how to start," I admitted, fidgeting in my seat across from her.

"Take your time," she said calmly, not bothering to turn her attention to the ding that sounded from her computer with a notification.

I rubbed my hands together and tried to get my heart to slow down.

"I'm sure you're wondering why I'm here without Elena," I laughed. "I doubt you ever expected to see *me* as a patient."

"I'm always open to new patients."

I blew out a shaky breath, wondering if it was a mistake to

come here.

"Does she talk about me?" I blurted out. I knew I didn't have to clarify who I was asking about. Hell, I knew that I shouldn't even ask in the first place, but part of me needed to know how much Elena had told her recently and whether Natalie was already judging me based on that.

"I'm not at liberty to discuss other patients."

I nodded, confirming that I knew that, yet it didn't stop me from pressing for more information.

"Has she seemed okay lately? I know you can't give me any details, but I just need to know if she's okay."

Natalie crossed her legs under the table and shifted in her seat as she continued to watch me.

"What makes you think that she's not okay?"

"I don't know..." I laughed. "Everything."

I knew that I sounded like I was losing my shit, and at that moment, I was.

"If you're concerned about her safety, then I suggest that you notify the proper authorities."

I continued to nod and folded my hands together in front of me as I stared at the floor. Why had I thought this would be a good idea?

"Why don't you tell me why you're really here, Trevor," she probed gently. "I can tell that something is bothering you. You wouldn't have called to schedule an appointment with me if not."

I forced myself to lean back in the chair, hoping that it

would keep me from jumping up and pacing the room.

She waited patiently for me to get my thoughts together.

"I think I'm losing my mind," I blurted out.

She reached forward and picked up her coffee mug, bringing it to her lips to take a sip before she set it back down.

"That must be a hard feeling to process and deal with."

I pulled my lips into a thin line and took a deep breath.

"Has anything happened recently that might be responsible for that feeling?"

"I'm sure you already know what's been happening from what Elena's been telling you."

"Why don't you tell me your side of it," she said, redirecting me.

I knew that no matter how hard I tried, she wasn't going to give me any insight into her sessions with Elena.

"Things have been different for a few weeks. Elena has seemed overly stressed, and as you know, we've all been worried that the anniversary of her kidnapping might be hard for her. She started acting weird, and we grew distant with each other for about a week or so—I can't remember how long. Anyway, she and I had dinner together the other night, and she mentioned some things that she insisted had happened between us, but I don't remember any of them. When I questioned her about it, she got really defensive and told me that she needed space."

"What kind of things?" Natalie asked.

I leaned my head back against the top of the chair and stared at the ceiling for a few minutes while I tried to remember everything she had accused me of.

"Some of them were random little things. Like me texting her when we were together. Or me following her on the subway when she was heading to her mom's house. But the one that got me the most was when she said that we had been intimate together and that I had tried to choke her."

I felt the color drain from my face as I swallowed down the bile that was starting to rise.

"I couldn't believe it when she told me about it, but she was so pissed off at me for not believing her that she insisted she could prove it because it was recorded on the camera that she had put up in her apartment. When we got there, the camera was still in the package, sitting on the coffee table. When I tried to talk to her about it, she freaked out and said that I was doing things to make her look crazy so I could be the hero and save her."

Natalie reached for her pen and jotted something down on a notepad before looking back at me.

"That is a lot to process, and I can understand the stress that you must be feeling. Have you talked to Elena since then?"

I shook my head and looked away.

"We both know Elena's past and why she would make a comment about needing to be saved. What I'm curious about is why *you* tensed when you said it. Your shoulders scrunched up, and you winced, which makes me feel like this might be part of the reason that you're feeling the way you are."

And there it was—the topic I had subconsciously been

hoping to avoid.

"Max went by her apartment yesterday and found a picture of my sister, Natasha. He didn't say how it got there, but he was pissed off about it."

"Did he say why he was upset?"

"He thinks that I'm doing things to Elena to make her feel crazy so I can save her."

She furrowed her brow and studied me for a moment.

"I'm not making the connection," she admitted.

"Max thinks that I'm trying to find a way to save Elena because I couldn't save Natasha. When we were growing up, she used to have terrible anxiety attacks that I would try to help her with. I do the same thing now for Elena."

"Why do you feel like you couldn't save Natasha?"

"She committed suicide. It was all my fault."

"I see," Natalie said quietly as she wrote more down on the notepad. "Why do you feel that it was your fault?"

"I used to have psychogenic blackouts when I was younger. I wouldn't remember anything that happened during them. Natasha started having her panic attacks around the same time and started to be afraid of me. Eventually, the blackouts stopped, and she and I got really close—she finally trusted me enough to let me help her with the anxiety attacks. Right before she died, her attacks started getting bad again—like really, really bad. I tried to help her, but she would freak out and yell at me not to come near her. No matter how hard I tried, she was convinced that I was trying to hurt her, not help her."

Natalie sat in silence for a few minutes while I blinked rapidly, trying to force the tears away before they could come out.

Finally, she spoke, her voice soft and gentle.

"When people take their own lives, it's never anyone else's fault. I understand that it feels like you failed her by not being able to save her."

My stomach churned as I sat up straight in the chair and looked her in the eye.

"What if it's happening again? What if I'm doing the same thing to Elena that my own sister accused me of?"

"What's that?"

"Tormenting her to the point of wanting to kill herself."

Natalie's eyes widened despite her attempt to keep the horror off of her face.

Twenty-Six
Elena
1 Day Ago

"What time is it?" I asked as I rolled over on the couch and glared at Max as his fingers flew furiously over the keyboard on his laptop.

"Early," he muttered without looking up at me. "Go back to sleep."

I flung the blanket off of me and swung my legs off the couch as I sat up.

"It's kinda hard to sleep when you're typing a mile a minute."

"I have work to catch up on," he said evenly as he stared at the screen.

Max had been at my apartment since I called him last night when I found the door open. It wasn't any surprise that he would rush right over, however, I hadn't expected him to pack up and move in. Or at least that's what it had felt like.

I got up and walked into the kitchen to start a pot of coffee when his phone rang.

"Romano," he answered, holding the phone between his ear and shoulder. "Okay, send me the video."

He pulled his phone away and set it on the edge of the chair beside him as he kept typing.

"What video?" I asked, not bothering to hide the fact that I had been eavesdropping.

"The one of your apartment. The site had crashed last night, so they weren't able to pull it until this morning."

The coffee pot was mid-air as I poured the water in when I stopped and stared at him.

"You have video on my apartment?"

"Yeah," he replied, still not focusing on me.

"Max!" I yelled angrily, forcing him to look over in my direction. "You put me under surveillance?"

"I needed to make sure you were safe." He closed his laptop and set it on the coffee table before getting up to join me in the kitchen.

"You should have told me."

"You would have told me not to do it."

I raised my eyebrows at him to confirm that he was correct with that assumption.

"Look, it's not a big deal. I have one camera set up outside to see who comes and goes."

"Is that the only one?" I questioned with my hand planted firmly on my hip.

He looked down and inhaled heavily.

"Max."

"There's one in your living room as well."

I picked up the towel that was hanging by the sink and

swatted him with it.

"Are you kidding me?! That is such a violation of my privacy! And I'm pretty sure it's illegal!"

"I was worried about you. I didn't know how else to make sure you were safe other than moving in with you, and Hannah told me that I couldn't do that."

"What if I walk around my apartment naked? Did you ever think about that?"

His face flushed an unflattering shade of red as embarrassment spread across it.

"I'm sorry," he said sheepishly. "I honestly never thought of you doing that until now, and it's not something that I ever want to think about again."

I narrowed my eyes at him and stepped closer, pushing my finger into his chest.

"What if Trevor and I were having sex in the living room, Max? I bet that's not something that you want to see either."

I paused for a moment and then smacked his arm.

"You're not even the one monitoring the video, are you?"

He shook his head.

"So who is the creep who has been watching me, Max?"

"He's a new guy. His name is Lucas."

I stepped away, needing distance from him as I tried to remember everything I had been doing in the living room the past few days. Had I done anything embarrassing?

Then I remembered the random stranger that had suddenly

been hanging out by my apartment.

"Is he tall and skinny, wears a leather jacket?" I asked through gritted teeth.

"So you saw him," he said, shaking his head in disbelief.

"He's been hanging out in the hallway directly across from my apartment."

He tilted his head back and closed his eyes.

"Fucking rookie."

"Well, maybe you shouldn't trust people you don't know to spy on your little sister and invade her privacy."

Max's computer dinged from the coffee table, and we both turned to look at it.

"That's the video," he commented before walking away to check it.

I followed and stood next to him so I could see over his shoulder. The video was short but showed a perfect picture of Trevor inside my apartment, coming from my bedroom with something tucked under his arm.

I leaned in to get a better view but couldn't tell what it was.

A few seconds later, another video popped up, showing the door from the hallway. We watched as Trevor walked out, not bothering to pull the door closed behind him. The guy who had been in the hallway wasn't there anymore. Trevor walked down the hallway and stood in front of the elevator while he waited for it. He turned to the side to check behind him, giving us the perfect view of what was in his hand.

I gasped and covered my mouth as I asked, "Is that my

blanket from Nonna?"

Max's shoulders tensed as he slammed the screen shut.

"I'm going to fucking kill him."

TEN SECONDS TOO LATE

Twenty-Seven

Trevor

1 Day Ago

After I left Natalie's office, I hadn't bothered to go to work. Instead, I texted Roman and let him know that I wasn't feeling well and would catch up on stuff this weekend. I locked myself in my apartment, trying to force the terrible thoughts out of my head that had managed to manifest and fester after talking to Natalie.

I had replayed everything that Elena had told me over and over in my head, trying to put the missing pieces of the puzzle together. If what she was saying was true, that meant that she wasn't the one we needed to be worried about. I knew that this day might someday come, but I hadn't stopped to think about what it would mean when it happened.

After Natasha died, I had sworn to myself that if I started having the blackouts again, I would leave and walk away so I didn't hurt anyone and make them suffer the way she did. The thought of no longer having Elena in my life was enough to burn a hole in my heart and make me wish that it had been me all those years ago instead of Natasha.

I was lying on the couch, trying to shut out the world, when I heard a knock on my door. I growled under my breath and willed whoever it was to go away. I wasn't in the mood to talk to anyone right now. Well, other than Elena. I would give anything to talk to her and fix things between us. The only problem was that I wasn't sure whether things were still fixable. I couldn't ask her to love me when I knew the power that I had to hurt her.

I closed my eyes and tried to focus on my breathing when I heard another knock. I muttered a curse word under my breath as I got up to answer the door. I flung it open, surprised to see Roman standing on the other side with a drink tray holding two cups of coffee and a brown paper bag from my favorite bagel shop.

The look on his face was one that I had seen a handful of times, and I knew that no matter what I said, he wasn't going to leave. I opened the door further and stepped to the side to let him in before closing it behind us.

"You didn't have to come by," I said grumpily as I resumed my spot on the couch. Roman quirked a brow at me as if that was the stupidest thing he had ever heard and set everything on the counter while he took his jacket off. A few minutes later, he was shoving a cup of coffee at me as he tossed the bag of bagels on the coffee table.

"Thank you," I smiled as I took the cup, forcing it to last longer than a few seconds. When had my life become so hard that it was nearly impossible to smile?

Roman sat down and looked around as he sipped his coffee.

"Eat your bagel," he instructed with a nod toward the bag.

"You're so demanding," I mumbled, reaching forward to pick it up.

"You get grumpy when you're hungry, and given that we're

going to have a talk that you don't want to have, I don't need you any pissier than you already are. So eat."

I rolled my eyes and took a bite, closing them for a brief second as the savory seasonings of the Everything bagel rolled over my tongue. It wasn't often that I ate a lot of carbs, but Everything bagels were my weakness.

Roman reached in and grabbed the other bagel. We ate in silence and finished our coffee before I got up to clean the mess. It wasn't that it bothered me to leave it sitting there on the coffee table; I just knew that I wasn't going to want to hear whatever Roman had come all the way over here to tell me.

Was he coming to scold me about my outburst the other day? Maybe it was to lecture me about being a better boyfriend to Elena? Or it could be about how shitty of a friend I've been to Max. The options were endless, and honestly, I already knew they were all true. It was hard to believe how much my life felt like it had unraveled in just a few weeks. It was like I blinked, and then everything was different, and I hated that.

I washed my hands, further stalling, then made my way back to the couch when there was nothing else that I could do to delay talking with him. I was a grown man, so I could always just tell him to fuck off and kick him out of my apartment, but I respected Roman too much to do that. He was a great friend, and if he was here, it meant that this was important to him. *I* was important to him.

I sat down and tried to force my rigid body to relax against the soft cushion while he looked calm and overly collected in his button-down shirt and dark denim jeans. The guys at the gym always joked that we were brothers from another mother because we were similar in so many ways—other than how we looked. Roman was tall, dark, and handsome and always dressed to impress. On the other hand, I was lighter-skinned, average height, decent looking, and usually lived in joggers and a t-shirt when I was at work—which lately was always.

He leaned into the side of the chair and studied me.

"I don't know what's going on with you," he admitted with a shake of his head, "but I'm worried about you."

I scrubbed a hand down my face and sighed.

"There's nothing to worry about," I lied.

"Bullshit."

I crossed my ankle over my knee and played with my shoelace to avoid meeting his eyes.

"It's nothing."

Roman leaned forward and rested his elbows on his knees.

"You're a terrible liar."

"What do you want me to say? That I fucked everything up? That I'm a shitty boyfriend and an even more terrible best friend? I'm well aware of how much I've screwed things up, and I'm going to fix them. Don't worry."

"Fix them how?"

"The only way that I can." I looked up and met his eyes. "By leaving."

Roman tilted his head back and let out a loud laugh which

irritated me more than it should. He thought this was funny? My life was literally crumbling around me, and he found it comical.

"Leaving," he repeated. "Because running away from your problems is really going to solve them?"

"With all due respect, you don't know shit about my problems. Trust me—leaving is the only way that I can fix this. It'll be better for everyone once I'm gone."

"Better for who? The girl who loves you and will be devasted when you ghost her? The best friend who has been there for you through some of life's hardest moments? Your mom, who has lost *every single person* she's ever loved? Me—your business partner who needs you to get your head out of your ass so we don't go under before the new year can even start?"

I raised a brow at him and pulled my mouth into a thin line.

"Business partner? When did that happen?"

"Today." He sighed dramatically and then added, "After I get done saving you from your damn self. You'll see how much you need me and offer me the position because you'll realize that you can't do this without me anymore."

I nodded and tried to keep the grin off of my face as he pretended to flick a piece of lint off his shoulder—*cocky bastard*.

"As much as I appreciate your concern, you have no idea what's going on. I'm not the man that everyone thinks I am. Elena might love me now, but she won't when she finds out who I really am. When she learns about the monster that lives inside of me, waiting to prey on someone as perfect as she is, she'll run and never look back if she's smart."

"How so?"

Flashbacks of Natasha trembling on her bed, crouched in the corner with a blanket tucked under her chin as she tried to protect herself with it flooded my brain. There was no other way out of this than to just admit the truth—I was a monster and didn't deserve to be loved by the people who had once trusted me.

"There are things about my past—things that I'm not proud of. It's part of who I am, and I can't change it, even if I wanted to. I don't want to hurt Elena, but that doesn't mean that I won't."

"We all have a past, Trevor. If anyone understands living with things that they regret, it's me. I've done things that no one should ever know about because it will haunt them and push them to the brink of insanity. If you're a monster, then that makes me one too."

"It's different, Roman. You did those things for our country, to protect us from people who wanted to harm us. You aren't a monster for that. You're a hero."

Roman chuckled and ran his thumb down the thin goatee that covered his face before locking eyes with me.

"I've taken people's lives from a mile away. They never saw it coming as the bullet ripped through their body, claiming their last breath. I hid in the darkness, lurking in the shadows as I planned my next kill. I waited for the perfect moment to end their life—not to spare them from the pain of death but to make sure that they felt *every agonizing moment* of it. I didn't afford them the comfort of quick and easy—I made it brutal and tortured them until the very last moment as I tried to make them feel an ounce of the pain they inflicted on their victims. Now tell me how you're a bigger monster than me."

The anger in his voice echoed off of the walls as his fists turned white from clenching them so tightly. He didn't talk much about his time as a sniper, and I knew that it was because it wasn't something that he enjoyed reliving. Some guys talked about their glory days or would brag about their sharpshooter skills, but not Roman. Those memories were enough to drive anyone to the depths of darkness that you could never come back from.

"My sister took her own life because she was being tortured and tormented by me. I have no memories of it because I used to have these blackouts. The only thing that I knew was what she or my brother would tell me had happened. My mother was a single mom who was working three jobs to try to support us, so she couldn't stop to get me the help that I needed, even if she wanted to. They stopped for a while, and I started to get close to Natasha. For a short time, she trusted me again. Then out of the blue, she started fearing me again. The next thing I knew, she put a bullet through her head and left a note that she would finally be free from me."

I pinched the bridge of my nose and forced my eyes closed as I tried to push the tears away. Reliving the guilt and grief of my childhood was too hard to deal with, which was why I constantly kept it locked up and buried as far below the surface as I could.

"Does Max know about your sister?" Roman asked, his voice lacking any of the judgment I had expected.

"Yeah, he was there when I found her. He tried to do CPR, but it was too late. She was already gone."

"So he knows about what happened with her and hasn't considered you a monster all these years—hell, he's even okay with you dating his sister. Why would you suddenly be a monster now if you weren't before? What's changed?"

That was the question that had been haunting me all day.

"I worry that I'm blacking out again and that Elena's been telling the truth about all of the things that she said I was doing. The things that I don't remember."

He inhaled heavily, his shoulders lifting then falling as he processed what I was really saying.

"I didn't mean to hurt my sister, Roman. I would have given anything to save her, and yet I'm the reason that she's dead. There's no way that I could live with myself if anything happened to Elena. She's been through enough already."

"I saw her yesterday," he blurted out randomly. "Elena," he clarified a few seconds later when the look on my face showed how confused I was.

"Where?"

"A couple of blocks away from work. I was heading there, and she came flying out of this building, looking frightened as she struggled to catch her breath. I asked if she was okay, and she said yes, but I could see on her face that she wasn't."

My heart ached, knowing exactly what he had seen. I hated that I hadn't talked to her lately and didn't know where she was coming from or why she was so upset. I wanted to pick up my phone and call her, just to make sure that she was okay, but I knew that I couldn't do that anymore. Those days were over.

"I was going to let her go on her way, then decided at the last minute to follow her, just to make sure she was really alright."

"Did she see you?" I asked, instantly pulled into the story.

He shook his head and frowned. "I live in the shadows, remember?"

I rolled my eyes and then nodded for him to continue.

"I followed her to her apartment and found something interesting."

He sat there with a smug smile, killing me with anticipation.

"What did you find?"

While part of me hoped that he would say that he had seen me there, another part of me cringed at the thought that this was all really happening. My mind still hadn't wrapped around everything at this point, and I found myself still clinging to the tiniest ounce of hope that there was another explanation for everything so I didn't have to say goodbye to Elena.

"Aside from the rookie cop posted up outside of her apartment and the cameras in the hallway, someone was in her apartment."

My heart leaped out of my chest as I leaned forward to hang onto every word. *Was it me? Please don't let me have hurt her.*

"Turns out that Max was in her apartment while she was gone. She hadn't even noticed the guy outside—I mean, if she did, she didn't seem to put together that he was assigned to watch her. I could hear her yelling at Max for scaring her, but she still didn't realize that she was being watched."

I let out the breath that I had been holding and tried to calm down.

"Did she know about the cameras outside?"

"No. I don't think so. Max didn't tell her about the cop either. He kept everything from her. She was more concerned with finding out about Natasha."

I pulled my head back in surprise and frowned.

"How did Natasha come up?"

"When Max was leaving, he found a picture of her and asked her where she got it. She said that someone left it for her and then asked him who it was. He told her the story but didn't go into too many details."

I swallowed hard, trying to push past the lump in my throat. She knew. She knew that I was a monster and what I had done. If I hadn't lost her before, I definitely would lose her now.

"What did she say?" I asked nervously. I wanted to ask *how* she got the picture of Natasha, but I was pretty sure that I already knew the answer when I looked over at the empty frame sitting on top of the mantel with the other frames. *How had I not noticed that it was missing?*

"That she finally understood what you meant about her not being the broken girl that couldn't be saved."

A single tear slid down my cheek as quickly as my thumb brushed it away.

"She wasn't afraid of you, Trevor. She *empathized* with you."

"Why are you telling me this?"

"Because you deserve to know the truth. You deserve so much more than you allow yourself to have. We all make mistakes, but that doesn't mean that we have to spend the rest of our lives paying for them."

I leaned forward and covered my face with my hands as the tears burned my skin with the grief they carried with them.

"I don't know what's happening with you and Elena," he continued as I tried to pull myself together. "But I do know that she's not afraid of you. Pissed off at you–probably–but not scared. I also know that Max cares about you, and even if he is ready to beat your ass right now, he wouldn't do anything to lose your friendship."

"I think it's too late for that," I laughed as I picked up my phone and read the text message that had just come in from him. "He's heading over here to talk to me."

"Well, whatever it is, I'm sure you guys will work it out."

"You don't know Max," I joked, suddenly feeling lighter than I had felt before he got here.

"Na, but my buddy Mike and I have been through some rough shit, and we always come out better than we were before."

"You have a friend who puts up with your crazy ass?" I asked, faking disbelief.

"Yup. We've been friends since first grade."

"That's a long time," I whistled. "Is he an only child? Is that why he bonded to you because he didn't have any siblings to harass him? Was he desperate for a friend?"

"Funny," he replied sarcastically. "He's the oldest of three kids, has two younger sisters."

"Well, take my advice—don't date either of them." I didn't bother laughing because I knew that sentence had more truth laced in it than I wanted to admit.

"No fucking way," he laughed. "He's in the FBI and works in the witness protection program. His job is *literally* to make people disappear."

I covered my mouth with my fist as a laugh erupted out of it. The thought of Roman being afraid of his friend was the comedic relief that I needed today.

"It's nice to see you finally laugh again," he commented as he stood up. "I'm here if you need anything, but do me a favor and fix things, so I don't have to. Talk to Elena, talk to Max. Fix your shit and get back to work because I'm not going to be partners with whoever this crazy version of you is." He twirled his finger in the air between us and then left.

While talking to Roman had helped lift some of the weight off of my shoulders, I still couldn't help but feel like everything around me was still getting ready to crumble.

Twenty-Eight
Elena
8 Hours Ago

Saturdays were supposed to be relaxing, but I had felt on edge ever since Max left my apartment yesterday. He went to talk with Trevor but hadn't bothered to give me any updates on what happened other than that it was *handled*. Whatever that was supposed to mean.

I threw a few slices of leftover pizza from last night into the microwave and waited for it to heat up. Today was going to be a stress-free day if I could help it. I had already taken a quick shower but didn't bother putting on anything other than my comfortable tights and a worn-out hoodie so I could lounge all day and do nothing.

My sisters had all taken turns calling and texting to see how I was doing and if I needed anything. Word got around fast in my family, and the drama was at an all-time high as they gossiped about the fight between Max and Trevor and—more importantly—who won. I hated feeling so out of the loop with everything, so I ignored most of the messages after confirming that I was fine and didn't know whether or not Trevor had a broken jaw. If they wanted to know, they could ask Max. That should keep him busy for a while.

The microwave dinged, so I took out my plate and headed over to the couch. I grabbed the blanket from the back and wrapped it around me as I got situated and turned on the TV. I wasn't in the mood for mindless TV, but I also didn't want the heartache of watching couples in love, so that ruled out any romcoms or chick flicks. The last thing I wanted to see was someone else getting their happily ever after when mine now felt so far out of reach.

I kept flicking through the channels until I landed on a true-crime show. My gut reaction was always to find something else to watch after what had happened to me, but suddenly I felt the need to push through and force myself to watch it. I used to love watching these shows before I was kidnapped and hadn't realized that I was still allowing Adam to have that power over me by not watching them anymore.

A commercial played as I took a small bite and chewed while my other hand was firmly wrapped around the remote in case I needed to change the channel. It was pushing boundaries and forcing me to take a step outside of the comfort zone that I had created right after everything that had happened. The one that forced me to be so constrained in this tiny bubble that even the tiniest thing could pop it. I was done living my life that way, and now was the time to change it.

I took another bite and accidentally bit my tongue when the show started, and an image of a house covered in crime scene tape filled the screen. My stomach twisted in knots as I tried to swallow the bite, my throat suddenly dry. I couldn't pry my eyes away from the TV as I reached over and picked up the glass of water from the coffee table.

A woman was narrating as they moved from the outside

of the house to the living room that had bloodstains across the walls and covering the floor. I turned my head away instinctively and shut my eyes, feeling my heart pound against my chest.

My eyes fluttered open, trying to adjust to the darkness around me with the only bit of light floating in through the crack in the wall beside me. My mouth felt swollen, and as I moved my tongue around, I could taste the bitterness of the blood on it. I tried to push myself up and felt my hand slip on something wet on the concrete beneath me. I rolled over and ran my finger in the liquid before lifting it to the dim light. Blood. I was lying in a puddle of blood, and I didn't know if it was mine or if it was from where I had cut him.

I felt my anxiety beginning to build and took a few slow, deep breaths in. I knew that I was in control of this and could change the channel if I wanted to. I was *not* the victim on TV. I was no longer the victim to anyone.

I opened my eyes and looked at the TV, relieved when I saw that it was a commercial again. It felt like I was torturing myself by doing this, but at the same time, I was tired of sharing my life with the demons that continued to haunt them. If I could learn to move past that trauma and accept it, then I would be more prepared to deal with it, so I could live a life where I wasn't constantly afraid of everything.

I finished eating one slice of pizza and lifted the other to take a bite when I heard my phone on the coffee table ding with a notification. I set the slice back on the plate and reached over to it.

Trevor: There will never be enough ways to tell you how sorry I am. I never meant to hurt you, and I will go to

my grave with the weight of knowing that I did.

I held my breath as I reread the text message. My fingers brushed across my lips to keep from instantly replying to his message and telling him that I forgive him and that we could work through whatever this thing was between us.

Instead, I exited the text message and set my phone back on the coffee table before wiping the tear away from my eye. I picked up my pizza and focused my attention on the show that had returned.

I knew that I needed to deal with things with Trevor but now wasn't the time. My heart wasn't ready for the trauma that was heading my way.

Twenty-Nine

Trevor

7 Hours Ago

My fingers flew quickly across the keyboard as I entered in the data from the reports that Roman had left on my desk. It was already after one in the afternoon, and I had what felt like eight shots of espresso to get me to this point. I had no idea how much I really had when the barista cut me off after six—who the hell cuts someone off of shots of espresso? Anyway—that hadn't stopped me from popping into the convenience store across the street to pick up a few energy drinks before making it into the office.

It was quiet for a Saturday with a few guys working out when I got here but quickly picked up a few hours later. I was thankful for the energy boost to help me crank out the work we needed to get caught up on before the end of the year. It was five days until Christmas, and my goal was to have everything wrapped up at work so I could take that week until New Year's off to spend time with my mom.

After losing both of my siblings, I knew that the holidays were always hard on her, but it was especially hard when Natasha decided to kill herself on Christmas Eve. Growing up, we always spent the days leading up to Christmas playing board games and drinking hot chocolate. My mom would nearly work herself to death by picking up extra hours to make sure she had enough money to get each of us something special for Christmas, while my dad was usually drunk and passed out in his chair by the tree.

He never cared about the holidays, and I don't think I ever saw him give my mom a gift for Christmas or her birthday. I could still picture her sitting on the floor between us three kids, her hands folded in her lap as she watched with pure excitement as we opened our gifts. Sometimes the gifts were more expensive than others, but there was always a look of fear in my mom's eyes when she would glance at my dad to see if he was watching.

It wasn't that he cared about what we got for Christmas. Hell, as long as he didn't have to pay for it, it didn't matter to him. But if he knew that she was working enough hours to be able to spend a lot on our gifts, his temper would flare, and he would beat her for keeping money from him.

I shuddered at the memory of her trying to stifle her screams from the bedroom as he threw her into furniture and called her every name in the book. I would try to distract Natasha, so she didn't have to hear it, though there was never a way to block it out. He was loud enough that the neighbors would hear, and eventually, someone would call the cops, or Mrs. Everly next door would come over and take us kids to her house, where it was safe. Not until I was an adult did I ever question why she didn't do something more to help my mom. She knew what was happening and yet looked the other way while telling herself that she had done a good thing by taking us out of the house.

I was ten the first time I decided to do something to save my mom. My dad had been drinking and had her pinned to the wall with the barrel of his shotgun held against her throat. Seeing her in that position had made my blood boil, and before I could think about it, I picked up one of her frying pans and swung it at his head. Unfortunately, I missed and got the beating of a lifetime that no one could save me from.

It wasn't long after that that I started having blackouts, especially when my dad would get mad. It felt like some sort of coping mechanism to protect myself from what I knew he could do to me. I hated that it made me feel weak and vulnerable because I could never remember what happened when I woke up. Soon my dad had taken a job out of town, and he started coming home less and less until one day, he just stopped.

We didn't hear from him again until after we turned eighteen, and he was no longer responsible for any child support—not that he would have paid it anyway. Then, finally, he came home and handed my mom divorce papers, threatening her life until she signed them. I remember once he left and slammed the door behind him that my mom sat at the kitchen table and cried. I had never seen her openly cry like that in front of us, and when I asked her if she was okay, she simply said, "I'm free. I'm finally free."

I was lost in my thoughts and hadn't heard my phone ding as I entered the last few pages of the report. Once it was done, I clicked save and leaned back in my chair, thankful that I had one big piece out of the way. There was still another week's worth of work to get done, but I had all day and night to work on it.

I pulled out an energy drink from the brown paper bag sitting at the end of my desk. I pulled the tab back and opened it, ready to fuel myself up for another work sprint. I knew that I would crash hard later, but right now, I didn't have anything else to focus on but work. I had texted Elena over an hour ago, and she still hadn't responded.

Not that I expected her to. What was she really going to say? *It's okay that you've been acting like a lunatic and making me think I'm going crazy, I still love you anyway!* Yeah, right.

Regardless, I said what I needed to, and I meant the apology I had given her. While I would have rather given it to her in person, that wasn't really an option. Aside from Max's not-so-subtle warning to stay the fuck away from his sister yesterday, there was still the fact that she had asked me for space and hadn't said that she was ready to see or talk to me again.

I picked up my phone and responded to the text message from my mom, confirming that I would be there for Christmas Eve. This year marked ten years since Natasha's death, and my mom wanted to go see her favorite play that they were putting on at the community center near where we grew up. She was buying tickets and wanted to know whether to get one for Elena.

It killed me to say no, that we wouldn't need a ticket for her. I was barely able to tell myself that it was over between us. I wasn't in any position to break my mom's heart even more right now. So instead, I lied and told her that Elena had to work that night, so she couldn't go. As far as I knew, it wasn't that far off from the truth.

Thirty

Elena

4 Hours Ago

"Thank you, ma, but I don't feel like going anywhere tonight." I balanced the phone between my ear and shoulder while I pulled my hair into a messy knot and secured a hair tie around it.

"Yes, I know that you're making manicotti," I sighed heavily, hoping she would get the hint. "But I'm tired and just want to stay home and relax tonight. I'll see you soon for Christmas."

My mom grumbled on in Italian for a few minutes before accepting that I wasn't coming over for dinner. I knew they were all worried about Trevor and I breaking up—had we really broken up, though? Anyway, I knew they were concerned and cared about me, but I didn't have the mental energy to deal with them tonight. I wanted as much peace and quiet as I could get.

I had spent the afternoon binge-watching *How I Met Your Mother* when I needed a break from the true-crime shows. I was proud of myself for watching as much as I had without having a full-blown panic attack. When I would feel myself slipping into one, I would focus on five things that I could see, four things I could touch, and three things that I could hear. I didn't have to get to the last two before I felt myself calming down, which felt like tremendous progress, though there was quite a bit of a sting every time I imagined that Trevor was here helping me through them.

No matter how hard I tried, I could not get him off my brain today. Hell—that was a lie. It wasn't just today. It was every minute of every hour since the moment he walked out of my door that day. Since then, nothing has felt right, and I wanted nothing more than to talk to him and fix things. Trevor felt like the air, and I didn't want to just take a breath — I needed him to breathe. He was my lifeline, and I felt like I was slowly dying inside without him.

I picked up my phone for the hundredth time and checked for any missed calls or text messages. I hadn't heard anything from him since his message earlier. I knew he was waiting for me to respond, but I didn't know what to say. I typed out different messages and then deleted them because none of them got the words out that I desperately needed him to hear.

You don't have to apologize. This isn't your fault. You don't have to be sorry for being who you are, I love you anyway. I'm not afraid of you—I know who you really are. Trust me, I believe in you. I love you. I need you. I don't want to live without you.

Against my better judgment, I picked up my phone and replied to his text message.

Me: We need to talk in person.

I knew that Max would be pissed off once he found out, but he should know Trevor better than to think that he would ever do anything to hurt me. Even I knew him better than that.

I got up and turned off the TV before heading to my bedroom to lay down for a bit. I put my phone on the nightstand beside my bed and curled up against the pillow as my eyes fluttered shut. Within minutes, I was asleep.

TEN SECONDS TOO LATE

Thirty-One
Trevor
1 hour ago

When Elena's text message came in, I was beside myself. I nearly choked on the water I was drinking when I read it. I had decided to switch to something *without* caffeine when I felt like I had reached the point of smelling colors and hearing numbers.

I responded quicker than I should have and let her know that I would be working late tonight but that I could call her when I got done. I hadn't heard from her since then, which had left me feeling uneasy that maybe she had changed her mind.

I thought about postponing the rest of what I needed to get done so I could rush over to talk to her, but that was what had gotten me into this predicament in the first place. I've never been so unfocused at work and never in a million years would have normally let things get this out of control here. My job was my life most of the time, and I took running my own business very seriously. I was ashamed that I had allowed it to get so out of control but was also grateful that Roman had put me in check before it was too late.

It was already seven, and my stomach was growling, asking for something more than liquid for dinner. I opened a new browser window on my computer and placed an order for delivery since I didn't want to stop and go grab something to eat. The sooner I got done with work, the sooner I could call Elena and see if she still wanted to get together and talk.

Once the order was placed, I minimized the window and returned to the other report that I needed to work on. I was busy entering the data when I heard my phone ding. I picked it up and felt my lips tug up in the corners with a smile when I saw Elena's name on it.

Elena: I just woke up from a nap, so I'm sure I'll be up late tonight. Let me know when you're done.

I let out the breath that I had been holding and shot back a quick confirmation message to her before turning my attention back to my computer. I was so focused on getting caught up on work to get out of there to see Elena that suddenly I wasn't hungry anymore.

"How much longer are you going to keep at this?" Roman asked as he stood by my desk and looked at the pile of paperwork that I had completed, which thankfully was larger than the pile I had yet to get done. I had been so caught up in it that I hadn't noticed him come in.

I pushed back from my desk and stretched. I was stiff and sore from leaning over my desk for so long and knew I needed to get up and move around soon. I looked at the clock on my computer and noticed that it was already after eight, and I hadn't bothered to stop to eat the dinner I had delivered. It was still sitting in the brown paper bag on the edge of my desk.

"I'm tapping out now," I sighed, pushing the papers away from me. "I'll come in tomorrow and finish the rest of it."

"I can do it this week, don't worry about it."

"I appreciate that, but you have enough work on your plate without adding mine. It's my fault that I got so far behind, so I'll make sure to get it done before I leave."

Roman nodded his head and tapped his finger on the stack of files that sat on the edge of my desk.

"How's your mom doing?" he asked.

I scrunched my face and shook my head. I felt bad enough that I hadn't been checking in on her more often than usual, but things had been busy, and she pushed me away every time I had tried. I knew that she was struggling with the holidays but this year felt like it was harder for her than it had been before.

"She confirmed that she got the tickets for the play and was bummed that Elena wasn't going to be there. Other than that, she hasn't said much."

"Have you talked to Elena?"

I felt a smile tug at the corners of my mouth and tried to remind myself that it didn't mean anything. She said she wanted to talk in person, and for all I knew, that was just so she could break up with me face-to-face and watch the agony on my face as my heart shattered around her.

"She texted me earlier and asked if we could talk. I'm supposed to let her know when I'm wrapping up here."

"Well then, I'll get out of here so you can go talk with her. Let me know how things go."

"Will do."

I returned his smile and started clearing my desk before shutting off my computer. I could feel the excitement bubbling inside me from the thought of seeing her again. I knew that Max had warned me to stay away from her, but I couldn't. She was like a forbidden sip of water when you were stranded in the middle of the desert. Sometimes it didn't matter whether you were supposed to have something if it was what you needed.

I picked up my phone and sent her a text message to let her know that I was done and to see if she wanted me to come over so we could talk. A few seconds later, my phone showed the bouncing dots on the screen as she responded.

Elena: Perfect timing. I'll be waiting.

I tucked my phone in my pocket and put on my coat. By the time I left, Roman had already shut down everything up front, so I didn't have to. I checked to make sure no one else was there before I set the alarm and locked the door.

It felt like it was going to take forever to get to Elena's apartment. My excitement to see her overshadowed any lingering doubts that I had that this wasn't going to go the way I was hoping it would. My connection with Elena was stronger than I've ever had with anyone before, so I refused to believe that our love for each other couldn't save what we had. I knew that I had my flaws, but I hoped that she would be able to see past them and remember why she had fallen for me in the first place.

As I sat on the train waiting for my stop, I caught my reflection in the mirror and shuddered when I saw myself. I didn't look like myself. The bags under my eyes, combined with the thinning of my face from skipping who knew how many meals this week, reminded me of my brother right before he died. Granted, he was using drugs at the time, but there wasn't much that differed between us now. I focused on my eyes, wondering if I could see the same evil in them that I had found in his so many times over the years.

The train jerked to a stop, and I got up. My illusions of happily ever after crumbled when my reflection looked back at me one last time, reminding me again why I wasn't good for Elena. It didn't matter how much I loved her; I would never be able to save her from the person who would hurt her and take everything from her.

Me.

TEN SECONDS TOO LATE

Thirty-Two
Elena

I chewed my nail as I clutched my glass of wine to my chest, unable to pry my eyes away from the TV as the woman desperately tried to run after the man who had taken her child. She was determined, but I could already tell that he was faster and stronger than her. That's how it always played out. No matter how strong the woman is, there's always a predator that will overtake her. My stomach soured as I thought back to when I had been kidnapped and held captive. I wasn't sure that I would ever escape; each day that passed made it less likely.

A knock on the door startled me, and I flung my arms in the air, sloshing the wine out of the glass. I gasped and set it down on the coffee table before I got up to grab a towel from the kitchen. I patted my arms and chest dry and then tossed the towel in the sink when there was another knock.

I looked through the peephole, my heart still racing from the movie. Whoever was there had their face turned away from me, keeping me from seeing who they were. I was about to walk away and grab my phone when they turned around, and I finally saw their face. Letting out a shaky breath, I turned the lock and slid the deadbolt to open the door.

"Hey, I thought you had to work late?" I stepped to the side and waited for him to come in. Instead, he lingered at the door with his hands shoved into his pockets, his jaw locked in place.

"Are you okay?" I asked, feeling as if something was wrong.

"Fine."

I pulled my head back slightly and tilted it to the side. Something was *definitely* different about him.

"Have you been drinking?"

"What's it to you if I have been?" His words weren't slurred, but the smell of whiskey was heavy on his breath.

"I'm just a little worried about you. You don't seem like yourself."

"Maybe I'm not."

"Did I do something?" I asked, narrowing my eyes in confusion. This wasn't like him and my skin prickled at the realization.

"I don't know. Did you?"

"What's with the games?" I asked, starting to grow impatient and frustrated. I put my hand on my hip and raised a brow. "If something's wrong, then just tell me. Otherwise, I don't know why you're acting this way." I was acting braver than I felt.

"Does it scare you?"

The icy tone in his voice was more jarring than his actual words.

"No," I said slowly. "You don't scare me."

He paused for a moment, studying me with cold, calculating, dark eyes. Something shifted between us, and I felt the icy chill radiating off him.

"Are you sure?"

Suddenly, my instincts kicked in, and I took a step back, away from him as he stepped toward me. My heart was racing as panic forced its way through my veins, sending me back into the darkness I felt when I was held captive last year.

I grabbed the side of the door, slamming it shut when he reached out and caught it. His hand wrapped tightly around the wood as he held it. His eyes locked onto mine, forcing a wave of fear to crawl up my spine. I took another step back, desperate to get away from him. He was inside my apartment now, the door still open.

"You're breathing fast. Eyes are dilated. I would bet that your palms are sweaty. Fear is coursing through your body right now, and you're trying to decide whether or not to trust *me* or your instincts that are telling you to *run*."

"Why are you doing this?" I whispered. He knew what I had been through; why would he think this was funny?

"So, which is it, *Elena*?" My name rolled off of his tongue in a way I'd never heard before. "Do you trust me, or are you going to run?"

"Stop it!" I demanded, my fists shaking at my sides. "Just go! Get out of my apartment! We're done." I pulled my shoulders back and tilted my chin up as my body trembled.

"Actually," he laughed, shutting the door. "We're just getting started."

I watched in horror as he slid the deadbolt in place, knowing that no one would be able to get in if needed. My head was spinning, and my body screamed for me to get the hell out of there and call for help, but it was too late.

"Trevor, why are you doing this?" I asked, my voice as shaky as my legs.

He took a step forward and worked his jaw back and forth.

"You haven't figured it out, have you?"

I stared at him, waiting for him to clue me in on what I was missing.

"Figured what out?" I asked, taking another step away from him.

"You were right, Elena," he replied, sidestepping my question.

"About what?" I didn't really care at this point; my goal was to keep him talking while I tried to figure out a way to get help. I looked around the room, trying to find something—anything that could be used as a weapon—when I suddenly stopped to focus on the bookshelf where Max had hidden his camera. At the time, I had thought it was funny that we had both picked the same spot to hide a camera, but now I was thankful that I knew where it was. All I had to do was get Trevor to turn around to face the camera so Max would see that he was here. Even if he wasn't actively watching—which it was Max, so he probably was—he would be able to go back and watch this later, and there would be proof that Trevor was there and had been doing everything all along.

"That I'm not acting like myself," he said with a shrug as if this was the most casual conversation to have. "I'm not myself, and you, out of all people, should know that."

I moved around in a semi-circle, putting my back to the bookshelf while I tried to position my body to where it wouldn't cover his. I needed Max to be able to see his face and get a good image of it.

"We all go through changes, Trevor. It's okay," I muttered, not entirely focused on the conversation. If Max was watching this live, I could give him a signal, and he would come save me. It was terrifying to think that I needed to be protected from Trevor, but the way he was acting left me confident that I was right to be afraid of him.

"Just to save you from that weird shuffle dance you're doing over there—the camera isn't there anymore. I took it down right after I disabled the ones in the hallway."

My heart dropped as the color drained from my face.

"You knew about those?" I asked, stalling while I tried to think of a plan B quickly. Of course, he knew; Max had probably told him when they were teaming up, trying to figure out how to protect me from myself. While it was true that I needed protection, I wasn't the threat anymore, and Trevor used that to his advantage to get information from Max that he wouldn't normally give away.

"I know everything, Elena."

There was something about how he kept saying my name that sent chills down my spine.

"Why are you doing this?"

Sweat beaded my brow as my blood pressure skyrocketed.

"Because there is something that I want. Something that I *need*. And unfortunately for you, there's only one way to get it."

"What do you need?" I gulped, afraid to hear the answer.

"Your boyfriend's dead body."

Thirty-Three
Elena

My phone rang for the third time in a row, much to Trevor's frustration. Not that there were many things that *didn't* irritate him right now.

I should have known better than to answer the door. I should have listened to Max's advice and stayed away from him. Instead, I was stupid and had texted him to see if we could talk. There was something about the idea of seeing him in person that felt so comforting to me that I was able to overlook everything else and let him in. Big. Mistake.

It felt like I had been sucked into a tornado, thrown into the thickness of the storm, as I stumbled around and tried to hang on to anything that would keep me from being swallowed into the chaos.

From the moment Trevor got here, he had been overly aggressive and controlling. Not much different than the few times I had seen him like this before, but definitely angrier. I was afraid of saying anything to make him even madder than he was. When he mentioned that he needed my boyfriend's dead body—I knew that he had reached a breaking point and had no idea how to handle it.

No matter how many times I've told him that I wasn't seeing anyone else, he didn't believe me. What was even worse was that he was now on a mission to find and kill this person that didn't exist. At first, I thought it was just jealousy at the idea that there might be someone else, but now I could see that there was something more. Something chilling and deadlier.

Twenty minutes after he forced his way into my apartment, he took my phone and refused to give it back to me. I should have been more concerned about it, but there wasn't anything that he could do that would be harmful at this point. If he thought he was going to text my *other boyfriend,* then he would have a hard time finding someone in my contact list, given that I had very few friends, to begin with. If he messaged one of my cousins, they would immediately alert Max and tell him that I was acting odd. Either way, Max would come to save me. I hoped.

For now, all I was focused on was staying as far away from him as possible and trying not to agitate him further. I didn't know how long I would have to wait this out, but I knew better than to do anything to make things worse.

I sat nervously on the couch, tucked into the corner with a throw pillow folded under my arm. An awkward silence fell over us as he paced back and forth in front of the TV, staring down at my phone.

All of a sudden, there was a knock on my door, startling both of us. My eyes widened at the clenching of his jaw as he stared at the door. Neither of us said anything. The ringing in my ears from the blood pulsing through was loud enough to drown out the sound of my heavy breathing while fear consumed me.

"Elena," Natalie called out from the other side of the door.

"It's Natalie. We need to talk."

I closed my eyes and felt the warm tears glide down my cheeks.

"I've been trying to call you, but you weren't answering, and I got worried."

Trevor turned and glared at me over his shoulder. I looked away, afraid to meet the icy-blue eyes watching my every move.

I stayed quiet, afraid that if I responded to her, it would set him off, and we both would be in danger. While there was a chance that she could run and get help, I wasn't willing to risk her life to try.

"I found your letter at my office today," she continued from the other side of the door. "I really need to see you and make sure you are okay. Please open the door."

The tears continued to trail down my face, burning my skin in their wake. *What letter was she talking about?*

"If you're not going to answer me, I have no other choice but to report this and call for a wellness check. I don't want you to be admitted, Elena. Please let me in. Let me help you."

Trevor rolled his eyes and grunted under his breath before nodding for me to answer the door. Once I got close to him, he yanked me by my arm and pulled me into him as he whispered in my ear, "Tell her you're okay and make her leave. If you say anything else—I will kill you."

I nodded and forced the bile back down as I tried to swallow past the lump in my throat. I quickly wiped the tears away with the backs of my hands and sucked in a deep breath.

I reached for the lock and slid it open when I felt something sharp prick the side of my throat. Carefully, I stepped back to crack open the door, the weight of the knife against my skin a frightening reminder not to let her in.

"Hey," I said as naturally as I could as I angled my face into the narrow opening so she could see me but not the knife. "Sorry, I was sleeping and didn't hear my phone."

Natalie pulled her brows together, concern deeply embedded in her face as she studied me.

"Can I come in?" she asked, tilting her head.

"Now isn't a good time," I said, trying to keep the anxiety out of my voice. "Can I call you later?"

"I would rather talk in person," she pressed. "Your letter has me very concerned."

I shook my head and blinked away the tears prickling my eyes.

"Is he here with you?" she whispered, looking behind me.

I closed my eyes and tried to force myself to be strong.

"Okay, well, I can tell that you're tired, so I'll let you go. Call me later?" Natalie said louder than she had been speaking before. She looked at me with empathy as she turned to walk away.

Before I could react, I was flung to the side, out of the way, as the door flew open. Natalie whipped around, her eyes wide with fear as she took in Trevor with the knife in his hand. In one swift movement, he grabbed her by the waist and threw her into the apartment, slamming the door behind him.

"You really fucked up now, doc."

I covered my mouth with trembling hands as I tried to hold in the scream as he backhanded her across the face with so much force that she stumbled before falling to the ground.

TEN SECONDS TOO LATE

Thirty-Four
Elena

I watched in horror as Trevor tightened the rope around Natalie's hands as he bound her to a chair in the corner. Her mouth had a cut on it, and streaks of mascara had run down her face. I sat beside her, tied to the other chair from my kitchen, useless and unable to help either of us.

When Trevor knocked Natalie out, I lost my mind and went after him. Seeing her lay lifelessly on the floor as blood pooled out of her head was enough to spark the fire that burned deep inside of me. I was only able to get a few punches in before he turned and pinned me to the floor with the knife pressed so hard against my throat that I started to bleed.

I kept my eyes on Trevor as he moved around the apartment, muttering about how he didn't need this fucking problem.

Part of me still hoped that Max would come to the rescue, but as time passed, it felt less and less likely that he would. If Trevor had disconnected the cameras, he wouldn't know what was happening anyway. And if he had assigned the rookie cop to watch me, he would probably assume that all was well unless he heard different. The same guy hanging out outside of my apartment for days was the same guy who suddenly seemed to vanish into thin air.

I tried to think of a way out of this but kept coming up empty-handed. It was impossible to do anything while bound to a chair, but it was even harder to try to negotiate with someone who you didn't know. Someone so full of anger and darkness that you were afraid to breathe the same air as them, just so you didn't risk allowing any of that darkness to seep into your soul.

My neck still stung from where the knife had cut me, but I had no idea how bad it was. I found Natalie's eyes linger on it every now and then, so I imagined that it probably looked bad if she was constantly checking on it. I couldn't feel the warm stickiness from the blood dripping down my chest anymore, so I had prayed that the bleeding had stopped for the most part.

Time seemed to pass by at a painstakingly slow pace as the threat of the unknown loomed over us. Trevor quickly checked the rope on both chairs before heading down the hallway and into the bathroom.

Once he was out of sight, Natalie turned to me as much as she could while being bound.

"I'm so sorry you got dragged into the middle of this," I whispered an apology to her.

She shook her head, and her face softened.

"I found a suicide note from you slipped under my office door. I rushed over as soon as I read it. Something about it didn't feel right, and I knew I had to check on you."

"Suicide note?" I asked. "I didn't write a suicide note."

"I can see that now," she sighed. "I should have seen the signs. I knew something was wrong last night and didn't trust my gut."

"What do you mean? What happened last night?"

"I ran into Trevor outside of my office. He was hanging out against the building and cornered me by the alley. He was different than he had been the day before when he came to see me. Angrier."

"He's been coming to see you?"

"Only once," she said quickly, looking past me to check if he was coming back. We stilled for a moment when we heard the toilet flush.

"I'll make this quick," she rushed out, "I think that Trevor suffers from multiple personalities, and whoever this one is—he plans to kill you."

I was about to respond when I heard footsteps coming down the hall. I snapped my mouth shut and pulled my spine straight, keeping the emotion off of my face.

Natalie closed her eyes and let her head rest lightly on her shoulder as if she had fallen asleep. I tried to take slow and steady breaths, hoping that my energy would somehow have magical powers that would help calm him down. Thankfully he seemed calmer than he had been, so I was hopeful that the *real* Trevor—the one I knew and loved—would be coming back soon.

He walked past and glanced at us before going over to the kitchen counter, where he had left my phone. Even if I had been quick enough to pick up the chair and hobble over to get it while he was in the bathroom, it was pushed so far back against the wall that there was no way to reach it with my hands tied behind my back.

My arms tingled from being restrained for so long, and I wondered if I would eventually start to lose feeling in them. He picked up my phone and started typing something before putting it back down on the counter. Then, seemingly satisfied with whatever he had done, he came over and sat on the edge of the coffee table, across from Natalie and me.

"All of this will be over soon enough," he said as if that was supposed to provide us with some sort of comfort.

"Please let her go," I whispered, nodding to Natalie. "She didn't do anything. Do whatever you want to with me but let her go. Please, Trevor."

"I can't do that." He rubbed his lips together and shook his head. "She already knows more than she needs to."

"I promise you, she won't say anything. She's a licensed therapist—her job is to keep people's secrets and help them find peace. She would never do anything to hurt me, so I *know* that she won't do anything if you let her go."

"It doesn't work that way. You should know that Elena," he laughed and rolled his eyes. "God, did you not learn anything with Adam?"

My heart stopped beating, and my blood turned cold when I heard his name on Trevor's lips.

"What did you just say?"

"Did you really think that you could survive him? You got lucky, Elena. He didn't come after you when you escaped because you weren't the one he wanted. If you were, you wouldn't have made it more than five feet outside of that warehouse. He was distracted and was an idiot who fell in love. Had it not been for Hannah, you would have had a different future. Or lack of one," he snorted.

"Fuck you," I spat out with more hatred than I had ever felt before in my life.

"You already did," he raised his eyebrows. "And honestly, it wasn't that great. You would think that a little choking might get you to put more effort into it; instead, you just lay there like a lifeless, terrified, limp fish. Honestly, sex with a corpse would have been livelier than what you did."

He pushed up off the coffee table and shook his head at me as if I disgusted him. I blinked away the tears and avoided looking at Natalie when I felt her gaze land on me.

A single tear fell from my eye, but this time, I didn't bother to hold it in.

TEN SECONDS TOO LATE

Thirty-Five
Trevor

I felt giddy and overly excited as I got ready. I knew exactly what I wanted to say to Elena and how I wanted to apologize for everything that had happened between us over the past few weeks. There were plenty of things that we needed to talk about and discuss, but none of that mattered until I could see her, hold her, and make sure she knew how much I loved her.

I knew that I didn't deserve her. Elena was the good in a world of evil. She was the light that brightened my darkest days. She was the definition of what love looked like and the reason that I didn't deserve to be loved.

One last moment with her was all that I would give myself. One last touch. One last kiss. One last time hearing her say *I love you* before I walked away and broke both of our hearts forever. To love her was easy. To stay with her could very well kill her.

TEN SECONDS TOO LATE

Thirty-Six
Elena

They say that you know when your time is up because you can feel death as it creeps closer, pulling back the layers that have protected you and made you feel safe. The icy cold that nips at your skin, drawing the warmth out of your body as you start to succumb.

Escaping Adam had been one of the defining moments in my life. It was when I realized that I was stronger than I had ever given myself credit for. I was smart, brave, and I had planned every move with calculated steps. There wasn't any room for error. If I slipped up, I would be dead, and I knew it.

Now with Trevor, things felt different. I couldn't push the feeling of death away from me. It covered me like a wet blanket, suffocating any lingering hope that I might survive this. But it was just a matter of time before I would be put out of my misery and free from the demons that continued to haunt me. Trevor was just one of many.

Natalie and I continued to sit in stunned silence, neither of us willing to try to talk to or negotiate with Trevor. It was clear that any leverage that I thought I might have had was long out of the window. There were a few times when I caught him looking over at me, and I saw a glimpse of the man that I used to know. The man who used to love me and cared about me.

My phone had dinged a couple of times with notifications, but there weren't any more phone calls after Natalie got there. I assumed that the messages were from Max and that he was probably starting to get aggravated that I hadn't answered. I no longer felt the excitement of him realizing that something was happening and rushing over to save me. It just confirmed what I've always known—I'm not the kind of girl who can be saved. *If* he got here, it wouldn't be in time. I already knew that.

I leaned forward and strained my eyes, trying to see the time on the clock on the stove. It was too far, and my eyes already hurt from crying so much that I gave up trying. It didn't matter what time it was, especially if my time on earth was ending soon anyway. I was tied to a chair, so it wasn't like I could go mark off items on a bucket list before I died. I was stuck here, at the mercy of a madman with some secret agenda that had yet to be revealed.

I wiggled my fingers behind my back, trying to get some of the numbness to go away. It was no use. *If* my hands were ever untied, they would just fall limply at my sides at this point. I wouldn't be able to fight back or even pick up my phone to call for help.

Trevor walked around the kitchen, setting things down on the counter, but I couldn't see what they were. Whatever he was doing, it was with purpose and determination as he pulled his brows together and focused intently.

I sighed heavily, allowing my body to relax into the chair as much as possible.

Suddenly, there was a knock on the door. I glanced at Natalie as her head whipped up toward the sound. We both knew that this was it if there was any chance of getting help.

It could be Max, or it could be the kids down the hall who were constantly doing some sort of fundraising for their school. It could also be my elderly neighbor coming by to ask for batteries for her remote that she fussed with a hundred times a day because her TV was never loud enough.

I held my breath and waited anxiously as Trevor walked over to the door, the knife tucked into his pants. He slid the deadbolt over, pulled the door open, and stepped to the side.

I gasped when I saw who was standing on the other side. The world spun around me as I tried to keep myself from toppling over in the chair as everything crashed around me.

Thirty-Seven
Trevor

"Elena?" I asked, confused as I saw her sitting in the chair with her hands behind her back. Before I could question what was happening, I looked to her right and saw Natalie sitting beside her in the same position.

I darted in, rushing over to them when I felt a strong hand pull me back. The door slammed shut, and then I felt the cold metal of a knife blade poke the skin on the back of my neck. I held my hands up in front of me and froze.

Elena looked bewildered as she looked between me and whoever was holding me at knifepoint. She looked like she saw a ghost as the color drained from her face. Natalie's jaw dropped open as she tried to process the same thing Elena was.

"Look, I'm not sure what you're here for—" I started to say before the knife pressed deeper into my neck.

"Shut the fuck up," a low voice growled. But it wasn't just any voice—it was one that curdled my blood and sent ice through my veins.

My body tensed, and my muscles stiffened in response. There was no fucking way.

I wanted to turn around and prove that this was all in my head. It wasn't the first time that I had thought I had seen my brother or heard his voice after his death, but every time it ended up being my mind playing tricks on me.

Just like now. I knew that Hunter was dead. I held my mom as she cried and grieved for another child so shortly after losing my sister. My mind was a dangerous place these days, and if I allowed myself to entertain the idea that it could be my dead brother, I would be climbing a slippery slope that had the promise of taking down everyone around me as I plummeted down it.

I tried to focus on the situation and pulled my thoughts away from the nightmares that haunted me. Unfortunately, now wasn't the time or place for that.

"Just tell me what you want. No one needs to get hurt," I said calmly, my hands still in the air by my head.

"It's a little too late for that," he chuckled.

I looked over at Elena, noticing the bloodstain on her neck for the first time. I had seen the gash on Natalie's head but had been too distracted with everything else to stop and focus on their injuries. *Were there more? What else had happened to them before I got here? How long had they been tied up and held hostage?* There were so many questions that I needed answers to.

"Look," I said, starting to turn around.

"That's enough!" his voice boomed as he shoved me forward.

I stumbled but quickly caught my balance, thankful that I was no longer in his grip. I turned around and held a hand to my neck, feeling the trickle of blood from where the knife had cut me in the scuffle. When I looked up, I felt my breath catch in my throat as my world came crashing down around me.

"No fucking way," I muttered, scrubbing my other hand down my face. I shook my head and took a step back, needing to put some distance between us.

"What's wrong? Afraid you've seen a ghost?" he mocked, waving the blood-stained knife in the air between us.

"You're fucking dead." I stepped even further back, running into the coffee table in the process.

I glanced over at Elena, confirming that I wasn't hallucinating and imagining my dead brother standing in front of me.

She was shaking as she sobbed, her body trembling against the chair.

"What do you want?" I asked, moving to stand in front of her. I hadn't been able to protect her before now, but I sure as hell would die trying from this point on.

"Your dead body."

TEN SECONDS TOO LATE

Thirty-Eight
Elena

No matter how much I wanted to scream, the sound wouldn't come out. I was frozen—paralyzed—with fear. Trevor stood there, staring at his *dead* brother, who wasn't dead after all. I couldn't imagine what he was feeling, but I imagined that it was a combination of shock and disbelief based on the way his jaw tightened as he worked it back and forth.

"What do you want?" he finally asked, folding his arms over his chest.

"I already told you." Trevor cocked his head to the side and narrowed his eyes. "Your dead body."

I felt a small gasp of air escape my lips. Everything made sense now that I was sitting there, watching them together. While they looked identical—because they were—there were so many differences that I noticed now that I was studying them. Trevor's body was usually more relaxed when he wasn't being held hostage by his dead brother, whereas Hunter's body seemed to constantly be rigid and tense. There was a light that shone in Trevor's blue eyes and lit up every time he smiled, which was the complete opposite of the cold, icy color of Hunter's.

"Fine," Trevor said, taking a step in front of Natalie and me. "But you let them go."

"I don't think so," Hunter chuckled menacingly.

"And why the fuck not?" Trevor bellowed, dropping his arms as he balled his fists at his sides.

"Because they're all part of the grand plan."

I wanted to lean around Trevor and see what Hunter was doing when I heard a noise in the kitchen. Trevor moved his body again, shielding my view before looking at me over his shoulder.

"Are you okay?" he asked quietly, looking between Natalie and me.

We both nodded but didn't say anything. He turned back to look at Hunter as he approached.

"Plans change," Trevor said firmly. "You're going to let them go, and then we'll deal with whatever the fuck you think this is."

"Do you really think you can stop me?" Hunter laughed and walked closer to us.

"We both know that you're not a killer, Hunter," Trevor replied calmly. "You wouldn't kill your own brother, so let's just step back and figure this out."

"Why wouldn't I? I killed Natasha."

Trevor flinched at the words, and before I could fully process them, I saw Trevor charge Hunter, tackling him to the ground. He swung hard, his fists repeatedly making contact with Hunter's face before he groaned and rolled over.

I watched in horror as blood puddled around him on the

carpet. He groaned loudly and clutched his hand to his side as Hunter pushed up and held the bloody knife in the air.

"Who's next?" he asked, looking between Natalie and me.

TEN SECONDS TOO LATE

Thirty-Nine
Trevor

"Get the fuck away from them," I yelled, forcing myself up off the floor as I kept pressure on the wound. There was blood everywhere, but I didn't have time to stop and worry about it. Elena was in danger, and there was nothing that I wouldn't do at this point to save her. If Hunter wanted my dead body, he could have it, but I would go to my grave making sure that Elena was safe.

Hunter stood behind them, slowly trailing the knife up and down each of their cheeks, leaving a trail of blood in its path. Elena pinched her eyes closed and cried while Natalie remained stoic. I knew that she had come across plenty of psychopaths in her profession, but I couldn't imagine that she had ever dealt with one in person.

I sat up, taking a slow, deep breath that hurt more than it should. I knew that I needed to find a way to call for help, but as I watched him untie Natalie, I knew there wasn't time. I was the only person who could stop him before it was too late.

"Let her go, Hunter," I commanded, pushing myself to a standing position. "You said you wanted my dead body, so let her go."

"Unfortunately, she's already seen and heard too much," he said with a shrug as he yanked her up from the chair after the ropes had been cut. Elena sobbed loudly beside them, her eyes wide with terror as she watched.

Hunter lifted the knife and held it against her throat as he pulled her hair, forcing her head back. She swallowed hard, and I watched the tears slide down her face.

"I'm so sorry," Elena whispered, rocking her chair to try to get free.

"Hunter, don't!"

I tried to dart over to grab her, but I was too late. The knife plunged into the side of her neck, and within seconds, the color drained from her face as the life slipped out of her body.

I closed my eyes and lowered my head as I heard the thud on the floor where she fell lifelessly in front of Elena.

Elena was crying so hard that no sound was coming out of her. Her body shook violently in the chair as she tried to get free. Before I could get to her, Hunter reached behind her and untied the ropes holding her down.

She jumped up once she was free and rubbed her hands over her wrists where she had been tied up.

Hunter took a few steps toward her as she rushed off to the kitchen. She looked around wildly before picking up a knife from the kitchen counter and pointing it at him.

"Stay the fuck away from me!" she yelled, her voice wavering as it echoed through the small room.

"Don't worry," Hunter assured her. "You're not next."

He stopped and turned to look at me.

"He is."

Forty
Elena

My hand trembled as I tried to hold the knife steady. I forced myself to focus on Hunter and not look at where Natalie was lying on the carpet, dead because of me. Had I not been seeing her, she wouldn't have gotten caught up in all of this.

I knew that I wasn't in any position to stab Hunter, but at the time, it was the first thing that I had seen on the counter where he had lined up a handful of different weapons. Some looked like they were purely there to torture someone, while others looked like they could kill someone if I put enough effort into it. The knife was shorter than the one he had, and I knew that he would stab me with his long before I got close enough to stab him with mine.

There wasn't much time to figure something else out as I watched Trevor clutch his stomach to try to stop the bleeding. He had sat down on the edge of the coffee table, unable to support himself anymore.

"Don't you come another step closer," I warned, shaking the knife at him.

"Why? What are you going to do if I do?" He licked his lips and took another step toward me. "You know that I like it when you're scared."

"Stop it," I hissed, looking from him to Trevor.

I kept walking, allowing my back to glide against the counter as I moved away from him.

"Did you tell him?" he asked, nodding to his brother.

I narrowed my eyes and pulled my brows together. He was trying to distract me, and I knew it, so I ignored his question and kept going, determined to make my way over to Trevor.

"I bet he just loved hearing about how good I fucked you," he prodded. "The way your pussy clenched so tight around my cock as you came. You were so fucking wet, and I knew that you liked being controlled, even if you fought it at first."

I tried to swallow down the bile that was rising in my throat.

I could feel every trigger being pressed as he kept talking.

"He was never very good in bed," Hunter continued. "His girlfriends in high school used to tell me how great I was when I would fuck them the way they wanted to be fucked. Trevor never could meet their expectations, so it doesn't surprise me that he didn't meet them with you either. He was always such a lackluster person in everything he did. Always so afraid to push the limits."

He shook his head and set the knife down on the counter.

I watched him cautiously, wondering why he would voluntarily give up the weapon he was using. I felt more unnerved and suspicious when he didn't reach for anything else.

"He isn't lackluster," I bit out, desperate to stand up for Trevor to his brother. "He's far better than you'll ever be."

Hunter tilted his head back and laughed.

"Maybe." He shrugged. "But the difference is that I take what I want. I don't sit around and wait for people's permission."

"What is it that you want?" I asked, hoping to keep him talking long enough for me to circle back around to get the knife.

"There are a lot of things that I want, but more importantly is what I *need*."

Your boyfriend's dead body.

"I don't understand," I said quietly. "Why do you need his dead body? There has to be another way to get what you want."

"There's not."

His tone was short and clipped, and I knew that the *friendly* Hunter I saw a few minutes ago was gone.

"So you're just going to kill your own brother?! You don't think people will ask questions and figure out that you killed him?"

"Nope," he replied, letting the p pop. "Because as far as anyone knows, he's still alive and well."

I pulled my head back, confused.

"Our father died a few weeks ago," he sighed and reached behind his back, pulling out a gun. "He left behind a substantial, very impressive inheritance. Fortunately for me, he never bothered to marry again or have any more kids, leaving one sole heir. And since I'm technically dead, that means that I need a new body so I can go claim it."

I covered my mouth with my hand and looked at Trevor.

"So you're going to kill your brother and pretend to be him?" I asked in disbelief.

"Exactly. Which means that I need to tie up all of the loose ends."

My heart was pounding so hard in my chest that it felt like it was going to explode.

"Loose ends?"

"I'm thinking a murder-suicide," he said whimsically. "Given the suicide note you left for your therapist and the ones still to be delivered to your family, the police will see that you weren't well and killed those who tried to help you. She was first," he paused and nodded to Natalie's body. "Then, when Trevor got here, you decided to kill him before taking your own life."

I shook my head, forcing the idea out as quickly as it came.

"There's no way you're going to pull that off. You can't make it look like I committed suicide," I argued. "The forensics team will look at the angle of the gun and rule it a homicide. No one would ever believe it."

"That's the funny thing about life, Elena. No one bothers to look that deeply when there's a suicide note. Trust me, I know."

"Natasha," I whispered as I sucked in a deep breath.

"Exactly. I made her death look like a suicide, and no one batted an eye. Of course, it helped that I had spent months tormenting her and accusing Trevor of doing it during his stupid blackouts. Dumb ass never bothered to do any research to see if it was even possible to do the stuff I accused him of while he was passed out on the floor like a total bitch. Add in a mom who is too busy to care about her kids, and I had the perfect situation lined up."

"Why did you kill your own sister?" I asked sadly.

"She was in the way, and she started to catch on to things that she didn't need to know about. I was getting mixed up with the wrong people, so I had to fake my death. I knew it wouldn't be long before she ratted me out and told my mom. I didn't need that kind of attention, and believe it or not, I was trying to protect my family from the people who would eventually come after me. I guess, in a way, I did them all a favor. Now it's time for him to do one for me."

He looked behind him at Trevor, who was barely sitting upright on the coffee table as his face grew paler.

"I think asking your brother to die so you can take over his identity is a bit much of a favor to ask," I bit out angrily.

His face hardened with anger. My pulse quickened as he lifted his hand and pointed the gun at my head.

"Like I said, I take what I want."

He turned and aimed the gun at Trevor. Before I could blink, I heard the sound echo through the apartment as a bullet whipped past me.

TEN SECONDS TOO LATE

Forty-One
Trevor

"Put your hands in the air and drop the gun!" Max yelled as he rushed into the room.

I was lying on the floor, all strength having left my body as I slid off of the coffee table and crumpled into a pile of uselessness.

"Now, Trevor!" His voice bellowed through the room, and I heard Elena scream.

Before I could get up to see what was going on, I heard another gunshot and tried to cover my head. It felt like being in the middle of a war zone as a few more bullets flew by before I heard a loud thud on the floor.

"NO!!" Elena screamed.

I struggled as I propped myself up on my elbow and saw her hovering over a body.

Blood spilled across the carpet, staining the beige a dark crimson in the process.

I looked around, trying to find Hunter when I saw Max lying on the floor in front of Elena. The door was open as the neighbors started poking their heads in to see what was happening.

I heard people screaming and yelling for someone to call 911. My eyes fluttered closed as I let my body fall back to the floor. If Max couldn't save Elena, then there was no way I would be able to.

Forty-Two
Elena

I sat stiffly in the waiting room chair, holding my head in my hands as I waited for an update on Max and Trevor. Last I heard, Max was still in surgery and had suffered severe damage from multiple gunshot wounds. Trevor was in the ICU, in critical condition from losing an extreme amount of blood as well as internal damage that had to be repaired in emergency surgery.

Back at my apartment, I had watched them carry Natalie's body out as a paramedic examined the wound on my neck. I was so numb at that point that nothing could hurt me. When they asked what my pain level was on a scale of one to ten, I had answered one hundred. This was a pain that I wasn't sure I would ever survive, and the only person I could talk to about it had just been brought out in a black bag tied down on a gurney.

My family lined the walls of the ER waiting room and comforted Trevor's mom as she cried in the corner, unable to believe the events that had unfolded. It was three in the morning, and no one was going to get any sleep until we knew that Max and Trevor were okay.

Hannah had taken the seat beside me as soon as she got there and refused to leave other than to use the bathroom or for an occasional drink of water. My mom was obsessed with trying to get me to eat something but the thought of putting anything in my body right now felt like pure torture. How could I eat when the two people I loved most in the world were lying in the hospital, fighting for their lives?

On top of everything that had happened, Hunter had somehow fled after Max shot him. Unfortunately, I didn't get a good view of where he had been shot, but I prayed that he was sitting somewhere in the dark, dying the lonely, painful death he deserved.

I felt like a terrible person for thinking that, but he really did deserve it, given the things he had done.

Roman had stopped by a handful of times with a guy I hadn't seen before. They spoke in hushed tones and scanned the room frequently. I had wondered if maybe he was someone that Roman had served with, but given the corporate-looking dress slacks and crisp button-down shirt he was wearing, he looked more like someone Max would work with.

It was surprisingly slow in the ER, maybe because the people of New York City finished up their violent crimes and murders earlier, or maybe it was just to torture me every time I heard footsteps coming down the hallway. My feet anxiously tapped against the yellow-tinged linoleum as I waited for an update.

"Any news?" Roman asked as he sat down beside me. The other guy stood next to him, arms folded across his chest as he looked around the room like he was guarding it.

I shook my head.

"This is my friend, Mike Sanchez," he said, nodding. "He's

going to help us find Hunter."

"Okay," I snorted. "Well, he better have superpowers if he wants to find him. He faked his death and lived in the shadows for years before he started pretending to be his brother, and no one noticed." I hung my head and closed my eyes. "I didn't even notice," I whispered.

"He doesn't have superpowers, but he does work with the FBI, and this is sort of his *specialty.*"

I looked up, taking in the dark gray eyes and strong jawline dotted with a thin line of trimmed hair. His jet-black hair was cut short and out of his face, giving him a professional look. Now that I looked at him, he had FBI written all over him.

"Nice to meet you," I said, extending my hand. "And good luck. He's going to be hard to find."

He gave me a curt nod before looking away. He didn't bother to reply, probably knowing that I was right. If Hunter had been able to stay under the radar this long, there wasn't much hope that we would be able to find him before he came back to finish what he started with Trevor.

"You know he will come back to kill him, right?" I asked, looking over at Roman.

He had been there when I told the story to the police and my family. It wasn't a secret at this point that Hunter had faked his death and was trying to take Trevor's identity to claim the inheritance their father left behind. While I wanted to believe that he would stop and give up now that his plans had gone sideways, I knew better than to trust a psychopath.

"We're counting on it," Roman confirmed, looking straight ahead of him as he pressed his hands together between his knees.

"While I want Trevor to survive this, it's terrifying to think he's safer if he doesn't. Who knows what extent Hunter will go to. He killed their sister and then had everyone believing that she committed suicide, for God's sake."

Roman sat quietly for a few minutes, thinking about what I said.

"Hunter is strong and determined," he replied quietly. "But even the strongest, most determined person cannot win against someone like Trevor. He has something that Hunter will never have."

"What's that?"

"A thirst for revenge."

Forty-Three
Elena

I sat in the pew as tears ran down my face, staining my face with grief. The priest led us in prayer, but the words never reached my heart. My mom reached over and squeezed my hand reassuringly as the choir began singing Amazing Grace. On the other side, my father handed me another tissue before blotting his eyes with his.

Their voices were beautiful, filling the church's walls as soft sobs echoed around me. Finally, the pallbearers headed to the front and began to carry the casket out. I lowered my head and allowed my body to shake as I cried.

Soon the song was over, and Natalie's body had been placed in the hearse. I knew that today would be challenging, but I hadn't imagined it would be this devastating.

The guilt I carried with me over her death consumed me. I hadn't eaten in the three days since it happened. I had no desire to do anything for Christmas, even though tomorrow was already Christmas Eve. My depression was at an all-time high, and I shot down every suggestion to find another therapist to talk to.

I waited until everyone left the church before making my way out. My parents had asked if I wanted to go to the cemetery, but I declined and knew that I wouldn't be able to handle it. I needed to say goodbye, and that was hard enough.

"Do you want to go home? I can make some risotto?" my mom offered as we walked to the car.

"I'm not hungry," I muttered, climbing in the back seat.

"You have to eat, Elena," she said with a heavy sigh. My dad got in and started the car, not bothering to get in the middle of what would end up being another fight.

I moved in with them a few days ago, in between spending most of my time at the hospital. Both Max and Trevor had yet to be released, and my days were beginning to blend together. It was probably due to the lack of sleep and forgetting to eat lately that kept me in this numb state of not caring.

Roman had provided a few updates from Mike on their efforts to locate Hunter. So far, he hadn't shown up at any of the hospitals or clinics in New York City, and Mike's team was unable to locate him on any of the traffic cameras in and out of the city. Just as he appeared out of thin air, he disappeared the same way.

Forty-five minutes later, we were back at my parent's house as the sun started to set. The neighboring houses were decked out with Christmas lights that seemed to sparkle in the fresh snow that had fallen. Our house was the only one with no lights and no hint of Christmas cheer. My family had been waiting for all of us kids to get together at the same time to decorate, and that never happened.

I ignored my mom's request to make spaghetti or lasagna as I took the stairs two at a time, desperate for some peace and quiet. It wasn't a secret that my mom and I bumped heads more than my siblings, but after being on my own for a few months, it felt like her overprotective mothering was constantly smothering me.

I shrugged out of my coat and gently pushed the door closed with my foot when I looked down on my bed. Lying on top of my pillow was a picture of Natasha that I had never seen before.

TEN SECONDS TOO LATE

Forty-Four
Trevor

"Take a deep breath. Again. Again."

The doctor continued to move the stethoscope across my chest while I struggled to keep up with the quick breaths she was asking for.

Finally, she pulled away and hung it around her neck before picking up my chart beside her. She scribbled something down before looking at me.

"How are you feeling?" she asked.

"Like I've been through hell and back," I replied bitterly. It wasn't her fault that I was in here or that I was cranky. After snapping at my mom and Roman, they left and gave me some space. It was a lot to process and take in, but that didn't make any of it any easier. Between Max still recovering from numerous surgeries and my psycho brother being on the loose, nothing was keeping me calm.

"I can imagine," she said sympathetically. "Your lab results look good, and your incision is healing nicely. We should be able to discharge you tomorrow, if not–Thursday."

"Merry Christmas to me," I joked, not finding any humor in it.

She smiled, but it wasn't as genuine as when she first came

in. After going through a list of what to expect over the next few days, she left, and I was finally alone. I thought about calling Elena, but I had no idea what I would say to her. She had been by earlier, but the room was packed, and we didn't have a chance to talk. Honestly, I was relieved that everyone was here because I wasn't sure that I would be ready to talk to her anytime soon.

I laid my head back against the pillow and closed my eyes. Part of me wanted to give in to the exhaustion that was clinging to me, but part of me knew that rest wouldn't be an option as long as Hunter was still out there. I wouldn't be able to sleep peacefully until I knew where he was—or better yet—until he was dead.

Not even ten minutes later, I heard a knock on my door before it opened, and Roman walked in.

"You up for some company?" he asked, popping his head through the narrow opening.

"Sure," I said, pushing the button to raise the bed back up to a sitting position.

"My friend Mike is with me. Is it okay if he comes in too?"

I nodded and then remembered that this was the friend that he was telling me about, the one in the FBI with sisters.

As they came in and shut the door behind them, I tilted my head and looked at Roman before asking, "Is he the one whose sister you're banging?"

Mike whipped his head around to glare at Roman, who immediately held his hands up in front of him and took a step back.

"What the fuck?" Mike growled, balling his hands into fists at his sides.

"Woah—you know I'm not screwing around with your sister," Roman said before looking past him to glare at me. "My friend Trevor here just has an ongoing death wish."

"Better not be," Mike warned, punching him somewhat playfully in the shoulder before coming in and taking one of the empty chairs beside my bed.

"Thanks a lot, mother fucker," Roman teased as he smacked my foot before taking the other chair.

"Hey, I needed some entertainment," I shrugged.

"Remind me to subscribe you to a porn site," he replied with a chuckle.

"No thanks, I'm good." I laughed, then immediately regretted it as the skin around my stitches pulled tight and made me wince.

"How are you feeling?" Mike asked.

"Good enough. These damn stitches are a pain in the ass, though."

"When do they think they can come out?"

"A few days, at least."

"That sucks," Roman said, leaning back in the chair. "Guess you'll be leaving all of the new clients for me to deal with while you handle all of the paperwork, *desk bunny*."

I closed my eyes and groaned. While I didn't necessarily love all of the new clients that came rolling in on January 1st with little motivation to actually work out, I loved paperwork even less.

"Haven't I done enough paperwork to last a lifetime just last week?" I complained.

"Hey, that was all your fault for messing it up, to begin with," Roman laughed.

"Well, I refuse to be stuck with all of it. Just wait and see—these stitches will be ready to come out in a day or two, and then I'll be healed and ready to go."

"Yeah, I don't think so." Roman shook his head while Mike tried to hide his laugh with a cough.

"Why not?"

"Because you're not Wolverine. You're a basic human who needs rest to recover."

"You sound like the doctor," I muttered, giving him a dirty look.

"Well then, I guess that makes me pretty damn smart." He winked and then propped his feet up on the corner of my bed.

"What do you think you're doing?" I asked, nudging his foot with my leg.

"Getting comfortable."

"For what?"

"You need to rest, and I'm going to hang out here so you can do so without any trouble."

I looked between him and Mike, noticing the gun attached to his hip for the first time.

"You're here to babysit me so I can sleep?" I asked.

Roman plopped his feet onto the floor and leaned forward, resting his elbows on his knees.

"Your brother faked his death then came back and tried to kill you and everyone you love so he could steal your identity to claim your dead father's inheritance," he said in one long breath. "So yeah, call it whatever you want, but we're not leaving until the threat has been handled."

"Threat?" I raised my eyebrows, wondering if they had any leads on where he was.

"As long as you're still alive, he's a threat."

I ran a hand through my hair, feeling the weight of the IV as it tugged under my skin, and pulled at the tape holding it in place.

For a moment, I felt relaxed, knowing that they would be there while I got some sleep. If I was going to face Hunter again, I needed to be at my best, which meant that I needed to build up my strength again. Just as I was getting ready to lay my head back, I felt a chill spread through my veins.

"I'm not the only one who's in danger," I said, closing my eyes. "He's going to go after Elena again."

Forty-Five
Elena

Silent Night played on repeat downstairs as my mom tried her hardest to lure me out of my room. I hadn't bothered to get out of bed despite my family's numerous attempts to feed me or get me to talk.

I hadn't bothered to tell them about the photo of Natasha that was waiting for me when I got home. It was also pointless to warn them of the impending doom heading my way. I knew that Hunter was just playing mind games until he could get me alone; that's why he left the picture of Natasha for me. Trevor was who he wanted, I was just a bonus, and I knew that he would kill me before he killed Trevor, just to make sure he felt every last bit of pain before he died.

It was oddly comforting to accept my fate and stop fighting the inevitable. Knowing Hunter was coming for me didn't scare me the way it should have. Maybe I was just too numb from everything that had happened, or maybe I had just reached the threshold of what any average person could withstand in a lifetime. In one year, I had suffered more loss and trauma than I had in my entire life. Hell, more than most people would in their entire lives.

I rolled over and pulled the pillow tighter into my stomach. It growled, a reminder that it lacked a basic necessity in life, but I didn't care. I had reached for my phone to call Natalie a handful of times, the ache in my heart deepening every time I remembered that she was dead because of me. A tear slid down my cheek, but I didn't bother to wipe it away. My skin was raw and irritated from a combination of the bitter cold and the constant crying I had done.

Hannah had texted me earlier to check in on how I was doing and let me know that they were keeping Max for a few more days. He had developed an infection that they were watching. She assured me that his partner Mindy had their team working with NYPD to find Hunter and bring him in.

I replied with a smiling emoji face and set my phone down. It was too much work to do anything else. Tomorrow was Christmas Eve, and whether I wanted to or not, I would be spending it downstairs with my family. I already had their gifts purchased and wrapped—though they were still at my crime-scene-ridden apartment—but the best gift that I could give them would be one last Christmas shared with each other before I was gone.

I thought about Trevor's mother and how hard the holidays must have been for her after Natasha killed herself—or rather was murdered—on Christmas Eve. The depths of grief and despair surrounding her family were immeasurable, and I would never wish that heartache on anyone.

She had been on my mind for days, and I had reached out several times to check in on her. She promised that she was okay and that her days were busy between spending time at the hospital with Trevor and picking up extra shifts at work to make up the hours she had missed.

My phone vibrated on the nightstand next to me, and I reached for it, not feeling an inkling of excitement until I saw the name on the screen.

Trevor: I'm getting released this afternoon. Maybe I can come see you so we can talk?

My heart started racing as my fingers flew across the screen.

Me: You should go home and rest, you need it. I can come by and see you when you're settled in. Just let me know what time, and I'll head over.

Trevor: I don't want you traveling by yourself.

Me: You're as much at risk as I am.

Trevor: I hate this.

Me: I hate it too.

I clutched my hand around the blanket and held it tighter to my chest as I waited for his next text to come through. I knew that he was worried about me going over there by myself, but I was even more worried about him. I barely suffered a cut to my neck where he had undergone several surgeries and still had stitches. It wasn't ideal for either of us to go anywhere by ourselves, but I also couldn't risk putting my family in danger by asking them to go with me.

Me: I'll be fine, Trevor. Let me know when you get home.

The dots bounced several times on the screen as he typed. I waited impatiently before his text message finally came through.

Trevor: Ok.

TEN SECONDS TOO LATE

Forty-Six
Trevor

"Do you need anything else?" Roman asked as he closed the fridge and joined me in the living room.

"I think I'm good, thanks."

I sat down, thankful that I wasn't as stiff as a few days ago. The stitches were healing quickly, and thanks to Roman and Mike hanging out in my hospital room so I could sleep, I felt better than I had in days.

Roman had escorted me home from the hospital and had groceries delivered, so I didn't have to go out to get them. Hunter was still out there, but no one had seen or heard anything since he fled Elena's apartment. Max's office chased several tips while NYPD went on wild goose chases that led to dead ends. He was playing games and enjoying every second of it while he scattered the resources that I needed to keep Elena safe. I could care less about my safety when I knew that I was the reason that we had to be worried about hers.

"Elena is still coming over?" he asked, leaning against the wall with his arms folded over his chest.

"I told her that I would let her know when I got home. I hate the idea of her coming here by herself."

He nodded and then pushed off of the wall.

"I'll take care of it."

I didn't bother to ask what that meant as he turned and headed out of my apartment, leaving me to peace and quiet.

We had checked the apartment when we got home, making sure that no one was hiding in the closets or under the bed. It felt silly to look in every nook and cranny, but it didn't stop the unnerving feeling that someone was watching me.

Forty-Seven
Elena

"Hey Roman," I said in a sing-song tone as I walked to the subway, throwing a glance over my shoulder. "You know you're not very stealthy. I saw you right away."

He laughed and quickened his pace to walk beside me. His hands were shoved in the pockets of the leather jacket that wrapped tightly around his muscular frame.

"I wasn't trying to hide," he stated with a shrug.

"So you didn't come all the way over to this side of town to follow me to Trevor's apartment?"

"No, I absolutely did that. I just didn't hide it."

I felt the corners of my lips turn up into a smile, and a wave of guilt washed over me. As quickly as it appeared, it disappeared. I turned the corner and kept walking until we got to the platform and waited for the next train to stop.

"It's okay, you know," he said casually as he stared straight ahead.

"What is?"

"To be happy." He turned his head and studied my face as tears pricked my eyes.

"Happiness is overrated," I muttered before the sound of the approaching train cut me off.

We rode in silence, not bothering to make conversation as people packed into the crowded space around us. I saw him scan the group plenty of times as he positioned his body to shield me on one side while my back was firmly planted against the wall, and an old lady sat on the other side.

After five stops, we finally reached ours. We waited for the people around us to move before he guided me out with one hand on my lower back. I let him lead me even though I knew the quickest way to Trevor's apartment. I assumed he was taking the long way to make sure no one was following us.

Once we were a few blocks away, I found Mike hanging out on the street corner, pretending to check something on his phone. I had seen Max do this plenty of times to know that there was nothing on his phone and that there were probably at least ten other undercover agents lined up around us. Roman's hand tightened against my body, and I felt him tense beside me.

Something was wrong.

Mike's jaw clenched as he slowly looked up and scanned the area around us. Suddenly, Roman pushed me to the side with my back against the wall as he stood in front of me and shielded me.

I desperately wanted to know what was happening but couldn't see anything past Roman's big frame. I heard voices around me as people passed by us, unaware of the danger lurking in the shadows.

"Where?" Roman asked, tucking his chin to his shoulder as he spoke. He was wearing a baseball cap that hid the earpiece until he slightly adjusted it so I could see. "Got it."

He slightly turned his head and whispered over his shoulder to me.

"He's here."

TEN SECONDS TOO LATE

Forty-Eight
Trevor

I had been waiting impatiently for Roman to get here with Elena when I heard the fire alarm go off. I jumped up—and instantly regretted it—and rushed to my bedroom, where the sound was blaring from. I waved my arm as I walked into a cloud of smoke.

My phone sat on the nightstand by my bed, plugged into a charger that was now on fire. I darted into the kitchen, grabbed the fire extinguisher from under the kitchen sink, then ran back in and sprayed it. Luckily the fire was out as quickly as it had started.

My heart was racing as I plopped down on the side of my bed, trying to ignore the throbbing headache from the alarm that was still screaming, and looked at the phone charger on the nightstand by the bed. Once the smoke had cleared, I leaned closer and saw the frayed wires that looked just like Elena's charger.

I had put my phone on charge after Elena had texted me that she was on her way but made sure that the volume was turned all the way up so I would hear if she or Roman called or texted. Unfortunately, my battery was almost dead, so I couldn't wait much longer to charge it. Out of everything that we checked when we got there, the charger wasn't on the list.

I knew that this was just the start. Hunter knew that I was home, and this was his way of letting me know that he was coming for me.

Forty-Nine
Elena

"What's going on?" I whispered into Roman's back as sirens blared around us, surrounding Trevor's apartment as we got closer.

"Fire alarm went off," he said stiffly.

"What?!" I gasped, covering my mouth with my hand.

Roman looked at his phone and guided me down the sidewalk, away from the people pushing past us.

"Trevor is okay," he confirmed. "He got out of the apartment and is heading to the gym. We can meet him there."

I exhaled heavily, letting out the breath that I had been holding. The gym was only a few blocks away, which meant that Trevor wouldn't have to go far before we could get to him. I would feel better once we were together, and I could make sure he was okay.

We were outside the gym twenty minutes later, waiting as Roman unlocked the door. He looked around before stepping to the side to let me in.

The lights were all off except for the one in the hallway that led to their office. Roman led the way, his gun drawn as we quietly approached the room. He stepped to the side and blocked the other end of the hallway while letting me slip inside the office. Trevor sat at his desk, his head back with his eyes closed.

I walked over to him, worried until I saw that he was sleeping. The angle he had his head in allowed us to see the cut on his neck. Knowing that it was Trevor, I took a few slow, steady breaths and walked quietly over to him.

Roman went through the rest of the office while I sat on the edge of the desk and studied his perfect face. It wasn't until my eyes traveled down his body that I noticed his hands tied together under the desk. He wasn't sleeping; he had been knocked out.

"You shouldn't be here."

I jumped up off the desk and whipped around as Hunter walked in, carrying a roll of black trash bags, duct tape, and a large knife.

"Stay away from me," I yelled, hoping that Roman would hear me.

"You need to leave."

My eyes felt like they were going to bulge out of my head.

"What the hell are you talking about? I'm not going to leave him here so you can kill him and steal his identity!"

"I don't have time for this, Elena. You need to get out of here and don't come back. Pretend like you don't know me and forget that we ever met."

"Stop it!" I yelled. "You're not going to get away with this, Hunter!"

"I'm not Hunter," he yelled, standing dangerously close to me as the heat radiated off his body. "Now leave and don't come back. I mean it, Elena."

"Don't fucking lie to me," I spat out, my hands trembling beside me. "I saw the cut on his neck, I know that's Trevor." I nodded my head to where he was still tied up.

"You mean this cut?" he asked, setting everything down on the edge of the desk before pulling his hoodie to the side and tilting his neck so I could see the cut. I narrowed my eyes, noticing it looked identical.

"I'm not going to tell you again, Elena—leave and don't come back. You're not safe here."

"I don't believe you," I cried out. "You're Hunter! You're just trying to get me to believe you, so I'll leave, and you can kill the man I love. I'm not going to let that happen!"

He stepped closer to me and locked his eyes on mine.

"If you love him, you'll do as I tell you to."

"Don't listen to him," another voice croaked beside me.

I turned my head to see *Trevor* waking up. He cleared his throat and blinked his eyes a few times.

"That's Hunter. Don't trust anything he tells you," he added.

I looked back and forth between them, unable to tell the difference for the first time. They were both wearing gray joggers and hoodies that matched.

"Shut your fucking mouth," Trevor number one growled in Trevor number two's direction as he squirmed under the desk.

"Enough," I said through gritted teeth. "I don't believe you," I said to Trevor number one as he stepped back from me and gave me some space.

"You don't have to. Just trust your gut Elena, what does it tell you?" he asked.

"It should tell you to run," Trevor number two behind the desk muttered. "I'm sorry I got you caught up in this. I didn't mean for you to get hurt."

I felt my heart pull at the tenderness in his voice. There was pain and sadness in his words which made me believe even more that he was really Trevor and not Hunter.

At that moment, I knew what I had to do.

I rushed over and ducked down beneath the desk, quickly working the rope around Trevor's hands until it was loose enough for him to pull them free.

I watched Trevor number one's jaw clench as he moved it back and forth.

"That was a stupid mistake to make," he growled so loudly that it startled me, and I jumped back.

"Stupid indeed," Trevor number two agreed as he got up from behind the desk and pulled a gun out of the bottom drawer.

He lifted the gun at the same time that Trevor number one lunged for him, tackling him at the waist and knocking the gun out of his hands. It fell to the ground and slid across the floor. I immediately rushed over and picked it up, remembering everything Max had taught me.

I quickly checked to ensure the safety was off before aiming it at them. The problem was that I had no idea who was who. *Where was Roman when I needed him?*

"Enough!" I yelled as they continued to wrestle on the floor. A few hard punches made contact with bone before I fired a warning shot into the window behind them and got them to stop. I wasn't worried about the broken glass or that someone might hear and call the cops.

They shuffled to their feet but not before one of the Trevors—how do you fucking keep them straight at this point—picked up the knife from the edge of the desk. In one swift movement, he grabbed the other Trevor and stood behind him with the blade pressed into his neck.

"Drop the knife now!" I demanded, feeling my hands slightly trembling. I gripped the gun tighter and widened my feet slightly to keep my balance.

"Shoot him, Elena!" Trevor yelled from under the weight of Hunter's arm as he held him in place—or at least that's who I assumed they were.

I looked between them, hoping for some sort of sign that I would know who the real Trevor was.

"Now! Shoot him!"

"That's what he wants, Elena," Hunter said, tightening his grip around Trevor. "He wants you to believe that I'm Hunter, so you'll shoot me, and then he doesn't have to kill me—you'll do it for him."

"No," I cried, realizing that was a possibility too.

"He won't stop until both of us are dead," he continued, holding the knife against his throat. "You know that. You saw it with Adam—*I'll kill a thousand people just to get to you*. Remember?"

Everything stopped around me for a split second as I thought about what he said. He was right; Adam wasn't going to stop until he killed me. He got distracted with Hannah once he had her, but I knew that he wouldn't stop until he brought me back and killed me. His words repeatedly played in my mind, but I had only told one person what he had said: Trevor.

"Don't listen to him!" Trevor cried out from under Hunter's arm. "Shoot him before he gets inside your head and it's too late!"

I closed my eyes for a brief second, praying that I would have some sort of divine intervention and God would help me to make the right decision.

When I opened my eyes, I heard a gunshot behind me and ducked at the last minute to avoid being hit. I whipped around to find Roman standing there, arms raised with his gun steady between his hands.

There was a loud sound as a body fell to the floor. I couldn't bring myself to turn around and see who it was. Instead, I dropped the gun I was holding and fell to my knees, covering my face as I cried.

"It's okay, Elena," Roman said from above me as he picked up the gun and tucked it into the back of his jeans. "He's okay."

"Elena!"

I felt strong arms wrap around and hold me tightly as my body trembled. I leaned into him, feeling the comfort I had only ever felt with Trevor. Roman was on the phone, notifying someone that Hunter had been shot and giving them the location.

I pulled away from Trevor and looked up at Roman as he stood guard at the door, waiting for the police to arrive.

"Where were you?" I asked, peeling his attention away from the hallway. Suddenly the anger that he had left me started to rise inside me.

"I was here the whole time."

"No," I shook my head and stood up. "I was in here by myself. You weren't here. Why weren't you here?" I yelled as I poked a finger into his chest.

He didn't flinch or pull away as I jabbed at him. Instead, he just stood there and let me have the breakdown I needed.

"I heard his voice and knew that he was here," he said calmly. "I work best in the shadows. If he knew that I was here, things would have gone differently."

"So you left me to handle things on my own?" I sobbed shakily.

"No, I just needed a few minutes to watch from afar so I could make a decision and confirm who was who."

I looked over at Trevor sitting at his desk with his shirt lifted as he checked to make sure his incision hadn't been ripped open in the scuffle.

"Part of my training included studying people and learning their mannerisms. You can tell a lot about someone from the way they act and what they do."

"So you knew which one was Trevor from the start?"

He nodded.

"I feel like the worst girlfriend ever," I groaned, blowing my nose into a tissue I swiped from the box on Trevor's desk. "I couldn't even tell them apart."

"I don't think many people would have been able to if they didn't know what to look for." He paused and looked over at Trevor. "For instance, Trevor has a small mole on his left hand, right above a scar he got when he was a kid. I didn't see either when Hunter was holding the knife. Plus, Trevor is left-handed, whereas Hunter felt more comfortable holding the knife with his right." I looked at Trevor's hand, noticing the scar and mole for the first time.

"Those are such small details to base such a life-changing decision on," I admitted.

"I agree," Roman sighed. "But I knew the moment they saw me. Trevor closed his eyes in relief, and Hunter narrowed his in anger. That was all that I needed to confirm what I already knew."

"Well, I'm thankful you were here," I said before we heard voices coming down the hall as the police arrived.

I moved to the side and sat down as they took over. For once, I felt like I could sit back and just relax.

Fifty
Trevor

"We don't have to do this," my mom objected as she lowered onto the plush chair the waiter held out for her, tucking her full-length dress underneath her as she sat down.

Once Elena was situated, I took my seat between them and pulled myself closer to the table. The restaurant was dimly lit with white Christmas lights scattered throughout, adding a soft ambiance to the quaint room. I pulled the linen napkin from the plate in front of me and laid it on my lap before reaching my hand over to rest it gently on Elena's thigh.

We hadn't had a chance to talk after everything happened yesterday, but neither of us seemed in a rush to have the conversations that we needed to have. Maybe we just wanted a peaceful Christmas Eve, or maybe we didn't need to talk out all of the gruesome details. Either way, things felt normal between us, and I wasn't going to do anything to change that.

I looked over at her, admiring how a thin strand of hair had fallen loose from the updo she had it in and framed her face. Her makeup was done in light shades of gray and silver to match the sparkles in the shimmery black dress she was wearing. She looked downright beautiful, and I found it hard to keep from touching her.

"Would you like to hear tonight's specials?" the waiter asked, standing at the head of the table with both hands behind his back.

I nodded but didn't bother listening as I continued to stare at Elena. She tilted her head back and laughed at something he said, and I realized just how much I had missed seeing her smile.

I looked up to find my mom watching me, a warm smile on her face. Once the waiter left, I took a deep breath and let it out. My mom knew what I was planning to do tonight, but it didn't make it any easier.

My fingers fidgeted under the table as I tried to expel some of the nervous energy I was suddenly feeling.

"Do you know what you're getting?" Elena asked my mother, briefly looking up from her menu to look at her.

"Everything looks so good I can't decide," my mom answered, lifting her menu so I couldn't see the shit-eating grin on her face. I was a nervous wreck, and she was loving every second of it.

"What about you? What are you getting?" Elena asked, lowering her menu to the table.

I swallowed hard and tried to think of an answer. Instead, I blurted out, "Will you move in with me?"

She pulled her head back in surprise, caught off guard by my random question.

I knew that there was a good chance that she would say no. She had already said no to my offer plenty of times before everything happened.

"I, um," she hesitated, and my heart sank.

I turned so quickly in my chair that it squeaked on the floor, drawing the attention of those around us. I offered a quick apologetic smile and then ignored them and focused on Elena. I reached for her hands and lined my chair up in front of her as she turned to face me.

"I know that you've said no before, and I get it," I said quickly. "But things are different now, Elena."

"How so?" she asked softly.

"When I first asked you to move in with me, it was because I thought *you* needed it. Now I'm asking you to move in because *I* need it. Because the thought of going a single day without seeing you drives me mad, and the idea of not holding you every night when you fall asleep causes my heart to ache."

She pulled her lower lip between her teeth and chewed it nervously for a few seconds before looking over at my mom and popping it free. When she looked back at me, she was smiling so big that it felt like it lit up the entire room.

"Yes, Trevor. I'll move in with you."

I pumped my fist in the air triumphantly before reaching forward and cupping her face as I pulled her in for a kiss.

"You just made me the happiest man in the world," I said between kisses.

"Congratulations!" Our waiter clapped his hands and squealed excitedly as he approached our table. He lifted a hand in the air, making a quick circular motion with his finger to another server, then took our order. A few minutes later, a bottle of champagne was delivered to our table as a gift from the restaurant to celebrate our recent engagement. We didn't bother to tell them that we weren't engaged as we toasted and shared this milestone in our relationship with my mom.

After he left, my mom leaned over and hugged both of us as tears of happiness filled her eyes.

"I'm so happy for you guys," she said, blotting her eyes with the linen napkin she had pulled from her lap.

"Thank you," Elena replied, gently squeezing her hand.

"It's about time we had something good happen," my mom joked, her face lighting up for the briefest second before falling with sadness. "Sorry, I didn't mean to ruin the moment."

"You didn't," I rushed to assure her. "It's okay to talk about things. A lot has happened in a very short time, and I know your head has to be spinning just as fast as ours."

The waiter came by to deliver our food before rushing off to another table.

"He wasn't always such an evil person," my mom said with her fork lifted in the air. "He was the sweetest boy until he started school. I still remember the day I got a call from his teacher, letting me know he had gotten into a fistfight with another boy and they needed me to come pick him up. I brought him home and sat him down, ready to give him a stern talking to before disciplining him, but your dad was home and took over instead."

She shook her head and let her shoulders fall with a heavy sigh.

"We didn't see eye to eye on much, but that was the first time I had ever stood up to him. Instead of disciplining Hunter for what happened, he gave him pointers on how to do better the next time. Something changed in Hunter that day, a darkness that shadowed the light I used to see in his eyes. After that, he became his dad's best friend and did everything he asked. I should have known then that he was going to be just like him, I just don't think that my heart was ready to handle it, so I pretended like I didn't see it."

"That had to have been so hard," Elena said, setting her fork down to listen.

"From then on, he was constantly getting in trouble at school, constantly fighting with other kids, defacing school property. Stealing," she sighed. "But then he started picking on Natasha, and I knew I had to do something. I tried to get him to go to counseling, but he refused. I tried every single method of discipline that I could think of, but nothing worked. It seemed like there was no way to get through to him. On top of that, I was working three jobs just to make ends meet, and even if I could find the time to help him, I didn't have the energy to do anything. I was constantly tired, and my depression was spiraling out of control."

"I'm so sorry, mom," I whispered, holding her hand. "I wish there was more that I could have done."

"When I got the news about Natasha, do you know what the first thing was that I thought?"

I shook my head but refused to let go of her hand. We had never discussed this before, and I wanted her to feel strong enough to keep going. I needed to know what my mom went through and the silent battles she faced that I couldn't see.

"I was so mad that she beat me to it."

The air left my lungs in such a rush that I felt lightheaded. My hand fell to the table, allowing hers to release from my grip. I looked at her with tears in my eyes, unable to believe what I had heard.

"When I saw how hard you were taking her death, I knew then that it had been Hunter who was tormenting her, not you. I knew that you would never hurt her, and seeing you in so much pain made me remember how much I loved you and how I would do anything to spare you that kind of pain again. If I could take it away, I would have."

She reached over and grabbed my hand again, giving it a tight squeeze.

"YOU are what kept me going, Trevor. You were my reason for living. You are the reason that I continue to get up in the morning and that I look forward to each new day. I miss your sister more than I could ever explain, but I know that she's free from the pain she was suffering as well."

"I had no idea," I said hoarsely, the tears burning my throat. "I knew that Hunter made my life a living hell, but I didn't know that he did the same to everyone else. I just thought it was because we were brothers, and that's what siblings do." I shrugged my shoulders and realized for the first time in my life that my brother was never the person I thought he was.

"I tried to keep as much away from you as possible. You didn't need that kind of negativity in your life. Once you met Max, I was soooo relieved that you had a best friend who would look out for you and protect you from the darkness surrounding Hunter. Shortly before his *death,* I had noticed some guys coming around the house looking for him. I knew then that he was in trouble, I just didn't know how deep he had gotten into it."

"Enough to dump his car in a lake and fake his death," I grunted. "I can't believe that he got away with it for so long."

"Max said that they found a fake ID he had been using. Apparently, he was already living someone else's life and looked similar enough to them that no one questioned it when he moved to a new city and started over. They're still looking for the guy's body he pretended to be before he came back here. The guy was reported missing by his family six months ago," Elena added. Max hadn't been able to say much, but this quickly became a massive investigation that spanned several different agencies and would likely take a while before it was wrapped up.

"Who knows how many other identities he's taken over the years," my mom said sadly.

"Or how many people he's killed along the way to get what he wanted," I said.

My mom and I had gone to the coroner's office this morning to identify his body. I've only ever seen a handful of dead bodies in my life, but the second I saw Hunter, I knew that it was him. Aside from the collection of new tattoos he had, everything else looked the same, including the birthmark on his back.

I leaned back in my chair and listened as Elena and my mom continued the conversation but felt distracted as I wondered if Hunter had gotten some of the tattoos he had because they were tattoos that the other person had before he took their identity. It wouldn't surprise me to see him be that thorough, just like it wouldn't surprise me if he had killed them as well.

Soon the conversation shifted, and we focused on eating our dinner before it got cold. Once we were done, we pushed our plates away and declined the waiter's dessert recommendations when there was nowhere to put anything else. We would be sitting for a few hours at the theater, and the last thing that I wanted was to be uncomfortable from overeating.

We got to the theater a little earlier than expected and took the time to talk to some of the people that my mom knew. We used to come to the theater a lot when we were little—when my mom could afford to bring us—and it became like a second home to me. Everyone was so friendly and took us in as their own when my mom wasn't around.

The lights flickered a few times to let us know the show was about to start. I grabbed Elena's hand and led her to our seats, smiling at my mom, who was already waiting for us. We sat down and enjoyed the show as a family, remembering and honoring my sister for the night.

Fifty-One
Elena

"That one is from me," I said cheerfully, rubbing my hands together excitedly as Max arched a brow and started to unwrap the small box on his lap.

He had been released from the hospital yesterday morning and was determined to make it to my parent's house for Christmas. Trevor and his mom had joined us, and I had never felt so happy before in my life.

I tapped my feet excitedly on the carpet, watching the red balls bounce on the reindeer noses on my socks in the process. Trevor wrapped his arm around my waist and pulled me into his side before planting a kiss on my cheek. I leaned into him, allowing my body to mold against his where it belonged.

Max tore the rest of the wrapping paper off and tossed it to the side as he examined the wooden box. He tilted his head and studied it for a minute, probably wondering if the box itself was the gift. It was a beautiful box, but it wasn't the real gift.

"Open it," I coaxed, waving my hand to encourage him to keep going.

He smiled and lifted the lid. I watched the emotions flash

across his face before he blinked away tears and looked at me as he covered his mouth with his hand.

Everyone waited impatiently for him to show them what was inside and had him so worked up. He wasn't a man who freely showed emotion, so this was a big deal.

He reached in and picked up a silver picture frame with the words *Superhero* written across the top with a picture of Max and me inside.

"Thank you," he said, his voice wavering. "But I'm not a superhero."

"Yes, you are," I protested. "And I'm sorry that I ever said that you weren't. You've been saving me since I was a little girl and have never let me down."

I let the tears slide down my face as we stared at each other and had a moment that only we understood.

"I love it, thank you," he said and gently put it back into the box.

"You're welcome." I smiled and laid my head on Trevor's chest as we watched my parents open their presents. They always went last, too excited to watch us kids open our gifts that they didn't want to miss out by opening theirs.

My mom thanked everyone as she made her way through the giant pile of presents until the only one that was left was from me.

I had struggled with what to get her this year. I put it off until the very last minute, stressing about how no matter what I got her, she wouldn't like it. She had everything she could possibly want or need, which left little room to surprise her with anything special.

Last night Trevor and I had decided to step into a store that was still open after we dropped his mom off for the night. I browsed the aisles, looking at the trinkets and figurines until my eyes landed on one that took my breath away.

I watched closely as she lifted the delicate sculpture out of the box and looked at it. It was a mother and daughter joined together by a heart that they were both holding. I knew the moment I saw it that it was the perfect gift for her and cried when I bought it. Even though we fought more than anyone I knew, it always came from a place of love, and I understood that now.

Her eyes welled up with tears as she held it, moving it around to look at every tiny detail. Finally, she looked up at me and smiled, holding it to her heart as a tear fell from her eye. *I love you,* she mouthed, and for once, everything in my life felt perfect.

TEN SECONDS TOO LATE

Fifty-Two
Trevor

"I still need to give you my gift," I whispered in Elena's ear as I wrapped my arms around her waist and pulled her back tight against my chest.

"Oh yeah?"

"Yup."

"Well, I still need to give you my gift as well. But unfortunately, it's stuck there until Max works his magic so I can get back into my apartment. I'm thankful that I had left most of my gifts here after I went shopping with my sister, but I hate that I didn't have anything to give you today."

"*You're* the best gift that I could ever ask for. But, if you want to go back to my place later, I can give you your gift then," I teased as my hands slipped down into dangerous territory, given that we were still at her parent's house. We had finished dinner, and her mom promptly kicked us out of the kitchen while she and Elena's sisters worked on cleaning up the dishes.

"We can go now," she offered, facing me.

I saw her grin pull across her face as her cheeks turned a slight shade of pink when she felt my erection through my jeans. Her hand drifted down my stomach and grabbed it, making me hiss in response.

"I thought you wanted to stay for pie?" I asked, closing my eyes while I tried to will my erection to go away.

"I have pie you can eat at your place."

"Let's go," I growled, spinning her around and gently pushing her toward the closet where our coats were kept.

She laughed and opened the door, pulling them out and handing mine to me.

"You guys outta here already?" Max asked, coming up behind us with Hannah.

"Yeah, I'm tired," Elena said as she shrugged into her heavy winter coat.

"Me too," I added even though I wasn't.

"You guys?" she asked, turning to face them once it was on.

"Same," Hannah laughed.

"Well, we can all sneak out at once, and then mom can't guilt us into staying. Strength in numbers, right?" Elena joked.

We said our goodbyes before leaving and taking the train back to my apartment. The ride was long as I thought about all of the things that I wanted to do to Elena once we got there. While I really did have a gift for her, it was the never-ending gift that I couldn't wait for her to open. The one where she rode my face until she came undone and cried out my name for all of my neighbors to hear.

As soon as we got inside, I locked the door and slid the deadbolt in place before stripping off my coat and helping her out of hers. Our mouths crashed against each other as we flung pieces of clothing across the apartment and stumbled our way to my bed.

She was naked except for a black lace bra and matching panties. I was wearing nothing but boxer briefs that already felt too tight against my raging hard-on. I hooked my thumbs in the sides and slid them off, allowing it to spring free as she climbed on the bed and looked over her shoulder with her ass in the air for me to admire.

"You're so fucking beautiful," I said as I stalked over to her and slapped her ass.

"Ow!" she giggled, wiggling it for me to spank her again.

I gave her a quick smack before rubbing the red spot, letting my fingers glide along the crack. Her back arched slightly before she spread her legs a little further, allowing me to go where I wanted to.

With one finger, I pushed her panties aside before running it down her slit, feeling the warmth and wetness from her pussy welcoming me. I played with her for a few minutes, teasing her before finally sliding my finger inside her.

She gasped and rocked down against my hand. I wanted to take my time and give her every ounce of pleasure that I could, but the way she was grinding against me told me that she was as ready for this as I was. I laughed as I slipped another finger inside and heard her moan in response.

She tossed her head, flipping her hair over her shoulder as she looked back at me. She chewed her bottom lip and rocked harder as she locked her eyes with mine.

"I want you inside of me," she urged.

"Your wish is my command."

I reluctantly pulled my fingers out and waited for her to get comfortable on the bed. I hooked my fingers in her panties and pulled them down her legs before tossing them to the floor. Before climbing on top of her, I grabbed a condom out of the drawer and put it on.

I soaked up the image of her lying in my bed– hair fanned out around her face with her full breasts pushed up on display in the new bra she was wearing. I glanced down, smiling when I saw the faint outline of the Christmas tree landing strip.

"Ho, ho, ho," I murmured before sliding inside her. "Santa's coming tonight."

She closed her eyes and moaned as I moved, lifting her hips to meet my every move. I trailed kisses along the side of her neck and down her collarbone before pulling the thin fabric down on her bra and taking a tight nipple into my mouth. I sucked hungrily, desperate for the release we desperately needed.

Sex with Elena was always great, but this time, it was different. It wasn't just the way she scratched her nails down my back or tightened her legs around me as I pounded harder inside of her, but the way that she opened her eyes and watched me as we climaxed together.

I had been worried that I had lost Elena forever, and now I was determined to show her every single second of every single day just how much she meant to me and never let her go again.

Fifty-Three
Elena
2 Weeks Later

"How are things going?" Hannah asked before pushing a french fry into her mouth.

I wiped my mouth and took a drink of soda to wash down my bite of pizza before I answered her.

"Good," I shrugged. "Different."

It was busy in the dining hall on campus, with students rushing around to grab a bite to eat before their next class.

"Do you like your classes so far?" She squirted more ketchup onto her plate, then looked at me while I thought about the question. It had only been a few days since I had started college again.

"I do," I said thoughtfully. "I think changing majors really helped."

She laughed and popped another fry in her mouth.

"Yeah, business is a lot different than psychology. But I'm glad that you're enjoying them."

"How are your classes going?" I asked, taking a bite while she talked. Her classes were very different than mine since she was still studying forensics, much to the dislike of my brother.

"They're good. I'm excited to be taking more advanced classes this semester."

We talked for a few minutes about school before she shifted in her seat and took a drink of water. Putting the cap back on the bottle, she looked around at the students scattered at the tables around us before turning back to me.

"How is everything else going?" she asked quietly enough for only me to hear.

I crumpled up my napkin and tossed it onto my empty plate while I finished chewing.

"Things are good. Living with Trevor is easier than I thought it would be. We finally got all of my stuff out of my old apartment and canceled the lease. My mom is just over the moon that Trevor and I are living together, and I think Max is relieved that he doesn't have to worry about me as much now that things are mostly back to normal."

"And you?" she pressed. "How are *you* doing, Elena?"

I knew what she was really asking, which was why I kept skirting around it.

"I don't know," I answered honestly, looking down at the table. "No matter how hard I try, I can't get past the guilt of knowing I'm responsible for Natalie's death."

The words burned my throat as they pushed their way through my mouth. It was something that I had thought about every single day but had never said out loud, but with Hannah, it was different because I knew that out of anyone—she would understand.

She smiled sadly but didn't say anything.

"Does it ever get easier?" I asked.

"No," she answered quickly, not missing a beat. "It's been over a year since Amber died, and I still blame myself for her death. Everyone has tried to tell me that it wasn't my fault, but at the end of the day, the fact remains that if she wasn't there at my apartment that morning, she would still be alive. Being my best friend is what got her killed."

Tears stung my eyes as I felt the pain in her words.

"Natalie came to check on me. She was worried about me because of the fake suicide note that Hunter left for her. If she wasn't my therapist, she would still be alive."

Hannah reached across the table and squeezed my hand.

"I know that it doesn't change anything, Elena, but I'm glad that you found someone that you were comfortable talking with. I hate that Natalie was murdered by a psychopath, but I can tell how much she loved and cared about you. If she didn't, she would have turned that letter over to the police and initiated a wellness check. She wouldn't have gone to see you herself."

"So you're saying that loving me is deadly," I joked, but neither of us found it funny.

"Not at all," she laughed and released me. "Bad things happen to good people all the time. Maybe we've just had our fair share, and now only the good things will happen to us."

She threw our trash in the trashcan next to us before picking her backpack up off the floor and sliding it onto her back.

"Are you heading to your next class?" she asked as I got up and grabbed mine.

"I'm actually done for the day."

My schedule this semester was super light while I tried to decide whether or not this was what I wanted to do—that and the fact that I had lost my scholarship and couldn't afford to pay full-time tuition. Trevor had offered to pay it for me, but I quickly declined his offer.

After NYPD and the FBI wrapped up their investigations and Hunter's real death was made public, Trevor had been contacted by the attorney who was handling his father's estate. He had considered refusing the inheritance, but when he thought about all of the years that his mother had suffered and went without so she could give them the best life possible, he knew that he should take it.

He had planned to pay off her house and deposit some into her savings account when the money came in. It was such a massive amount that he would be able to do everything he had been saving up for at the gym AND still have enough left over to retire. But Trevor was a hard-working man with a drive and determination like no one I had seen before. It meant a lot to him to own his own business, and he wasn't going to let a large sum of cash change that for him. As far as he was concerned, he still worked a forty-hour workweek and paid his dues, just like everyone else.

Hannah and I said goodbye and went our separate ways as she headed to class, and I headed home. *Home.* It felt weird to say that, but I honestly never felt more at home than at Trevor's apartment. From the time we started dating, it was the only place I was comfortable besides my parent's house.

Now that everything had settled down and we didn't have endless interviews with law enforcement, I tried to find my groove again. I stopped by the store on my way home to grab some groceries to make dinner tonight.

When Trevor got home, I had chicken baking in the oven and a spinach salad ready in the fridge. Trevor was always better at eating healthier than me, so I was learning new ways to cook now that I lived with him, but that didn't stop me from saying yes to my mom's invites for a carb-heavy dinner every week. Even Trevor didn't complain about her fresh garlic bread and rigatoni when he joined me last week.

"Honey, I'm home," he teased, shutting and locking the door behind him. He set his keys down and shrugged out of his coat before finding me in the kitchen.

I was standing by the stove wearing nothing but a black apron that barely covered my breasts and was just long enough to hide the black lace thong underneath.

"Fuck. Me." He leaned against the doorframe, rubbing his finger across his jaw while chewing his lower lip.

"Oh, trust me—I plan to."

I winked and turned seductively, popping my ass in the air to give him a full view as I opened the oven and pulled the chicken out. As soon as I had it set down on the trivet, I felt Trevor's hands slide across my ass and pull me to him. I tossed the towel to the counter and allowed his hands to roam over my body.

He pushed my hair to the side and then untied the apron, letting it fall to the floor. I turned around, covering my breasts with my hands as his eyes clouded with lust.

"Dinner's ready," I said innocently.

He growled before pushing me up against the wall and crashing his mouth down over mine. Our tongues danced around each other as his hands worked the zipper on his jeans. I heard the sound as they fell to the floor and knew that he was as eager to fuck me as I was to be fucked.

He lifted me by the waist and pinned me to the wall before pulling his cock out of his briefs and sliding my panties to the side. I arched my back to give him better access as he plunged inside of me, not having any resistance given how wet I was.

I closed my eyes and dug my nails into his back as he plowed deeper inside of me, fucking me as hard as he could against the wall. I opened my mouth to moan, but his mouth captured the sound as he kissed me harder.

I could hear the picture frames rattle as he moved his hips faster and harder, sending me over the edge with each move. His finger slipped down between us and rubbed my clit, giving me the push that I needed as he came inside of me. We both climaxed simultaneously, neither of us bothering to stifle our moans at that point. His neighbors had given up on complaining about how loud we were after they realized that there wouldn't be anything that stopped us from constantly going at it on every surface in his apartment.

Once he was done, he lowered me to the floor and made sure my wobbly legs would hold me before he let go.

The smile on his face was so fucking sexy that I couldn't get enough of it. I wanted to see it all day, every day. And thankfully, that's exactly what I got now that I lived with him, and we were back to humping like rabbits.

Right after Christmas, we had both gone for an annual check-up and decided that we would both get tested for STDs given that I had accidentally slept with his brother—something neither of us would ever talk about again for the rest of our lives. At Hannah's urging, I took a pregnancy test when my period was later than usual. It turned out that mine was late because of stress, and hers was late because my brother couldn't keep his hands off her. I was excited that I was going to be an aunt, even if I wasn't allowed to tell anyone about it yet.

Now that we both had the all-clear from the doctor, we did it every chance we got without bothering to use condoms. Trevor and I both loved the feeling without them, and I was still on birth control until we decided that we were ready for that level of commitment. Moving in together was a big enough change for me right now, so I didn't see any babies in our near future.

We cleaned up, and I threw on some yoga pants and a t-shirt before we sat down to eat. The chicken was still plenty warm after our quickie, which worked out nicely. We sat on the couch and watched TV for a bit before Trevor set his empty plate down on the coffee table and looked at me.

"So, I was thinking," he started nervously.

He rubbed his hands together, and a faint blush crept up his neck.

"About what?" I asked, setting my plate down and trying to keep the panic out of my voice. *Was he already regretting having me move in with him? Had he gotten bored with our sex life and wanted to spice things up?* My mind was going a mile a minute, worrying over the tone he had used while his anxiety spread from his restless legs to mine.

"Roman and I were talking about this guy he's been seeing. He's really good, and Roman likes him a lot—"

My eyes went wide with surprise before he realized what he was saying.

"No, no," he laughed. "For therapy, Elena. Roman has a guy he's been going to for therapy."

"I'm not judging," I laughed, holding my hands up in front of me.

"Very funny," he mocked, laughing with me. "Trust me, Roman has women lined up waiting for him, and he has never had a problem saying no."

I raised my eyebrows, but it didn't surprise me. He was incredibly handsome with a muscular body that women obsessed over.

"Anyway—I was thinking about going to see his therapist."

My heart fluttered, and I put my hand to my chest. This was a huge thing for Trevor, and I felt so honored that he was talking to me about it.

"Yeah? I think that would be great!"

Something that looked like relief washed over him as he leaned back against the couch.

"I was wondering if maybe you'd like to go with me to a few sessions? Like couple's therapy?"

His voice caught again, and now I knew why.

We had talked several times about this, but it was always

about whether I was going to find someone new to see. Natalie's death had jaded me in more ways than one, but the thought of going to therapy and talking about the last therapist that I got killed felt like too much for me. *What if they thought I was bad luck or started to fear me because of what happened to Natalie?*

I swallowed and thought about my words before I said them.

"Hannah and I talked today at lunch," I started. "I asked her if it ever gets easier—dealing with the guilt of knowing that you're responsible for someone's death."

He flinched and closed his eyes.

"She said that she still feels guilty about Amber's death and that it hasn't changed for her a year later." I paused and took a steady breath. "I know that Natalie's death isn't anything that I'm ever going to forget or just *get over*. But I also know that I benefited tremendously by seeing her after everything happened with Adam. She helped me heal in ways that I didn't know how to heal on my own."

He smiled, but his body was tense again as he waited for my answer.

"I think therapy could be great for you, our relationship, and me."

He raised his brows in surprise.

"I think it's time that I find a new therapist as well."

It was something that I had thought about all afternoon after Hannah and I had talked, and I realized that not going to therapy wasn't going to change what happened to Natalie, but it could impact what happened to me. I felt stronger when I was seeing her, and I knew that I could find that strength again if I pushed myself to get the help that I needed. Grief was a brutal beast to handle, but I owed it to myself to try.

Epilogue
Trevor
6 Months Later

"How are you not melting in that?" I asked Max as I tugged at the tie that was way too tight around my neck.

He chuckled and shook his head. The song changed as the wedding party took its place at the front of the church. Tears filled his eyes as Hannah started down the aisle, her white lace dress wrapped tightly around her swollen stomach. I felt a knot in my throat as I watched them, knowing that someday I wanted this for Elena and me.

I leaned forward slightly and caught a glimpse of her wiping her eyes while trying not to drop her bouquet. She was the maid of honor, and I got to be the lucky one who walked her down the aisle since I was the best man. It was hard not to imagine us up here instead, but I knew that she wanted to go slow and for now, moving in together was a big enough step.

"You look beautiful," Max whispered to Hannah as he graciously took her from her mom. She planted a kiss on Hannah's cheek before taking her seat in the front row, next to my parents.

The ceremony was short and sweet–just what the happy

couple had wanted and what I needed so I could get my hands on Elena again. It was summer in New York City, and the short rose-colored dress that she was wearing begged for me to slip my hand underneath it as soon as we had a moment alone.

We had gone six months with condom-free sex and only had two pregnancy scares along the way. Elena was the one who was scared, whereas I was the one who was disappointed with each negative pregnancy test. I hoped that someday she would want to settle down and have my babies, but I also kept reminding myself that while I was thirty, she was barely twenty and still had her prime party years ahead of her.

After smiling until my cheeks ached, the wedding party was finally released so the photographer could get some pictures of just the bride and groom before the reception. I took the first opportunity that I had to sweep Elena away and make our way to an empty staircase.

"I've been waiting to do this all damn day," I growled as I pinned her against the wall and slipped a hand between her thighs. I planted kisses along her jaw and then down her neck, stopping myself before I tugged the top of her strapless dress down to gain access to her nipples.

"We just had sex this morning," she laughed, not bothering to stop me as I slid a finger inside her. She gasped and let her head fall back while a moan escaped her lips.

"I will never get enough of you," I replied, moving another finger in while rubbing her clit with my thumb.

"Good, because I'm kinda addicted to you," she said breathlessly, moving her hips to grind against me.

"Especially with the daily orgasms."

I felt the strain against my trousers as my dick pressed against them, eager to be free and mark her as mine. There wasn't a time or place when I didn't want to fuck Elena, and her newly increased sex drive was working in my favor.

"Right there," she murmured into my shoulder before biting down to stifle her moan.

I rubbed harder, knowing exactly what she needed to get her there. I felt the first spasms a few seconds later as her orgasm ripped through her and her legs trembled against me.

I pulled my hand away and smiled down at the beautiful woman in front of me.

"They're going to start looking for us soon," she laughed, fixing her dress as I stepped away to give her some space.

"We better get back out there and pretend to be the best damn best man and maid of honor they've ever seen," I laughed.

We snuck down the stairs and joined the wedding party right before they were being led into the ballroom for the reception. Given our roles, we were supposed to be in line behind Max and Hannah, so it was painfully obvious we had been missing when they gave us their not-so-subtle glares as we stepped in behind them.

"Where have you two been?" Hannah whispered to Elena as Max's jaw clenched.

"I needed a drink of water," Elena lied, looking away as her face flushed red.

"You still look dehydrated," Max commented. "Your face is

red and splotchy, and your skin looks sweaty. How far did you go to find water? There's a fountain right there." He pointed to the one across the way from us in between the restrooms.

I was about to answer but snapped my jaw shut when the wedding coordinator person—I had already forgotten her official title—snapped her fingers to get everyone's attention before leading us into the room—saved by the bell.

The doors opened, and an upbeat song played that we all danced our way into the room to. It was fun and lively, and I felt the weight of the world lifted from my shoulders as I watched Elena laugh and smile as I twirled her around the dancefloor before leading her to her seat. I took mine next to Max and prayed that he wouldn't pepper me with any more questions about where we had been or what we were doing. If anything, he should know by now not to ask.

The DJ spoke into the microphone with an update on dinner being served when Max leaned over. I felt my phone vibrate in my pocket and pulled it out.

Before he could ask any questions about Elena, he noticed the frown on my face and nodded to my phone.

"What's up?" he asked.

I read the message again, furrowing my brow.

"It's Roman," I said slowly as I reread it. "He needs time off from work."

"What's going on? Is everything okay?" he asked.

"No, I don't think so," I said as I typed out a reply and waited for him to respond.

A few minutes later, I got his text message:

Roman: Quinn and Rosie are missing. I won't stop until I find them.

I looked at Max, a look of concern passing between us when we knew what that really meant. It wasn't just a random kidnapping; it was an innocent five-year-old who had no chance of surviving her captors without some sort of miracle.

****

Ready for more? Grab Roman's story, Against The Clock and be sure to pre-order Mike's story, Out Of Time!

Against The Clock https://books2read.com/u/m2YwoR

Out Of Time https://books2read.com/u/4DKMoP

TEN SECONDS TOO LATE

Acknowledgments

I would like to thank the loud voices in my head that keep me up at all hours of the night, telling me stories and demanding that I write them down. Without you, I wouldn't have a strong caffeine addiction—heeelllooo coffee!

I'd also like to say thank you to my wonderful alpha and beta readers for helping me through this one—Azucena, Niki, Amanda, Stephanie, and Katy—thank you so much for your feedback along the way and for helping me to make this story what it was.

Thank you to all of the readers who took a chance on this story and any of my others. I hope you enjoyed the story and that I allowed you to escape into an alternate—yet kinda scary—world for a little bit. I appreciate all of your support and the friendships that I've made along the way.

To my parents and sister, thank you for the constant love and support with everything that I do. You make me feel like it's possible to move mountains to get to what I want.

Richard, my wonderful husband—fifteen books in and I'm still as grateful for your help as I was with the first book. We've come a long way together on this journey and I love that you haven't abandoned me along the way. I love you so much and thank you for supporting my dream!

To my girls—even in the midst of chaos—like moving into a new house—you can reach your goals and achieve your dreams if you just keep trying. Don't ever give up, even when it feels impossible. I love you both with all of my heart!

TEN SECONDS TOO LATE

About the Author

Samantha lives in the southwest with her husband and two small children after abandoning her childhood dream of living in a cabin in Colorado when she found that she couldn't afford to live there and was deathly allergic to the woods. When she's not writing she's usually spouting off sarcastic remarks while drinking wine out of a coffee mug to look like a functional adult while chasing down her toddlers. She enjoys spending time with her family, watching reruns of Friends, and the 24/7 flow of coffee that can be found in her veins. Be sure to follow her on social media for updates on what she's working on.

You can find her here:

Facebook: https://www.facebook.com/AuthorSamanthaBaca

Instagram: https://instagram.com/author_samantha_baca

Goodreads: http://www.goodreads.com/authorsamanthabaca

Facebook Reader Group:
https://www.facebook.com/groups/2945710968775398/

Webpage: https://authorsamanthabaca.wordpress.com

Newsletter: http://eepurl.com/g0NcSj

TEN SECONDS TOO LATE

Other Books By Samantha Baca

The Haven Brook Series:
'Til Death Do Us Part (Haven Brook Book 1)
https://books2read.com/u/m2RJNR

The Cradle Will Fall (Haven Brook Book 2)
https://books2read.com/u/b6O0QE

The Ties That Bind (Haven Brook Book 3)
https://books2read.com/u/mqgoz8

A Very Haven Christmas (Haven Brook Book 4- Novella)
https://books2read.com/u/mvqGjj

Three Strikes, You're Gone (Haven Brook Book 5)
https://books2read.com/u/mvqL2z

The Dark Shadows Series
Five Steps Ahead (Dark Shadows Book 1)
https://books2read.com/u/38Q0gO

Ten Seconds Too Late (Dark Shadows Book 2)
https://books2read.com/u/3JRgVB

Against The Clock (Dark Shadows Book 3)
https://books2read.com/u/m2YwoR

Out Of Time (Dark Shadows Book 4)
https://books2read.com/u/4DKMoP

The Stone Creek Series (Novellas)
Chocolate Covered Mistletoe (Stone Creek Book 1)
https://books2read.com/u/3LRk9N

Candy Coated Promises (Stone Creek Book 2)
https://books2read.com/u/mldP5Y

Pumpkin Spiced Possibilities (Stone Creek Book 3)
https://books2read.com/u/bojdwV

Standalone Books
One Last Wish
https://books2read.com/u/mqg7D9

Finding Love In Apartment 2C (Novella)
https://books2read.com/u/bze9aZ
Cocky Counsel: A Hero Club Novel
https://books2read.com/u/31Kzkn

Holiday Books
Snow Place To Go
https://books2read.com/u/4A560N
A Christmas Wish
https://books2read.com/u/4EKXpE

TEN SECONDS TOO LATE

Made in the USA
Columbia, SC
21 January 2025